1985

University of St. Francis
GEN 891.71 P987t
Pushkin, Aleksandr Sergee
The bronze horseman :

W9-ACT-639

The Bronze Horseman

The Bronze Horseman

Selected Poems of Alexander Pushkin

Translated and Introduced by
D. M. Thomas

THE VIKING PRESS   NEW YORK

LIBRARY
College of St. Francis
JOLIET, ILL.

Translation, Introduction and Notes copyright © 1982 by
D. M. Thomas

All rights reserved
First published in 1982 by The Viking Press
625 Madison Avenue, New York, N. Y. 10022
Published simultaneously in Canada by
Penguin Books Canada Limited

"Eyes wide open, the poet weaves..." and "Invocation" appeared
originally in *Grand Street.*

LIBRARY OF CONGRESS CATALOGING IN PUBLICATION DATA
Pushkin, Aleksandr Sergeevich, 1799–1837.
The bronze horseman.
I. Title.
PG3347.A2   1982   891.71′3   81-70186
ISBN 0-670-19241-4   AACR2

Printed in the United States of America
Set in Palatino

891.71
p987+

CONTENTS

117, 434

II · Narrative Poems and Dramas

ACKNOWLEDGEMENTS

I have four authors to thank for leading me to a belated appreciation of Pushkin. First and foremost, John Bayley, to whom I am grateful not only for his brilliant comparative study, *Pushkin* (Cambridge University Press, 1971), but also for his personal advice and encouragement. This is but the latest of many debts I owe him. I am grateful to John Fennell for his admirable selection from the poet's work, with prose translations (*Pushkin*, Penguin, 1964). Where I have sought a fairly literal tone, I have been much influenced by his lucid prose versions. Henri Troyat's biography, *Pushkin* (Allen & Unwin, 1974), gave me an overwhelming impression of the poet's life, his aliveness. Here, too, I came across free-verse translations of love poems (rendered from Troyat's French by Nancy Amphoux) which moved me far more than any metrical versions I had read. This suggested to me that for certain of Pushkin's poems free-verse might be the most faithful form of translation. Finally, I wish to add to the chorus of praise which greeted Sir Charles Johnston's elegant and sparkling version of *Eugene Onegin* (Penguin, 1979). Pushkin described translators as 'the post-horses of enlightenment'; Johnston's *Onegin* is the first post-horse from east to west bearing authentic news of Pushkin.

D.M.T.

INTRODUCTION

1

I n his memoir *The Oak and the Calf*, Solzhenitsyn describes the fateful moment when, as the unknown author of a tale about the labour camps, he walked towards the offices of *Novy Mir*. Questions jangled in his head. Why had they summoned him to Moscow? Was it a trap? What compromises would they try to force him to make? As he crossed Strastnaya Square, he paused by Pushkin's statue, 'partly to beg for his support, and partly to promise that I knew the path I must follow and would not stray from it. It was a sort of prayer.'

Apart from the coincidence that both owed their education directly to the Tsar of the day – Pushkin at the imperial *lycée* founded by Alexander I, and Solzhenitsyn in the labour camps founded by Stalin – the two great writers seem to have little in common. Yet Solzhenitsyn's words make it movingly clear that his act of pausing by the statue was more than a pious gesture to a dead poet; that it was, in a sense, a real conversation – as though the poet were *not* dead. And for Russians he is not. This is something other than the immortality of all great artists. Pushkin is more alive to Russians than Shakespeare or Wordsworth is to us.

'Pushkin is one of the phenomena that live and move eternally,' wrote the critic Belinsky after the poet's death. There was some quality in his genius which allowed him to live in the future as well as the present. He would create an image, a person, or a new form – create it perfectly, even if he thought he had merely experimented – yet still leave so much unexpressed life that his collected works have become a kind of notebook, bursting with ideas, for later Russian authors to use. Eugene Onegin, the 'superfluous' man, went on living and growing in Turgenev's novels, and, more sinisterly, in

Dostoyevsky; Tatiana moved on also, into Turgenev, and into Tolstoy's Anna Karenina. The mysterious Petersburg of 'The Bronze Horseman' goes on glittering and shimmering in Gogol, Dostoyevsky, Blok, Bely, Akhmatova; the humble hero of that poem stumbles on through Russian realism, beginning with Gogol (Pushkin, indeed, literally gave Gogol the ideas for *Dead Souls* and *The Inspector General*). The blizzard in his poem 'Demons' blows still in Dostoyevsky's *The Devils*, Blok's 'The Twelve', Akhmatova's 'Poem without a Hero', and Pasternak's *Doctor Zhivago*. It is less a question of influence than of a still-living force, a wind that hasn't blown itself out, a continuing miracle of loaves and fishes.

He almost needed to die young in order to leave his successors with work to do. It would have been immodest for him to have lived longer.

He was born in Moscow on 26 May 1799, to parents who lived the frivolous life of the minor aristocracy. His precocious gift became obvious during his schooldays at Tsarskoye Selo, near Petersburg. After leaving school, he divided his life between artistic creation and dissipation, initially in Petersburg, and then in southern Russia. He was sent there, on the Tsar's orders, so that he could purge himself of the liberal sentiments of some of his poems. Officially it was a government posting, for Pushkin was nominally a civil servant. In reality he philandered, took pot-shots at the bedroom ceiling, wrote poetry while lying on the billiard table, and drank in the wildness of the Caucasus. In 1824, after three years at Kishinev and Odessa, he offended the authorities again and was consigned to virtual house-arrest at his parents' estate of Mikhailovskoye in north-west Russia. His absence from Petersburg during the Decembrist uprising in 1825 almost certainly saved him from the fate suffered by many of his friends: perpetual exile to Siberia. The new Tsar, Nicholas I, summoned Pushkin to Moscow and questioned him personally. As a consequence of this meeting, the poet was allowed to come out of exile and to live and publish 'freely' in Moscow and, later, Petersburg. Pushkin's freedom proved illusory; he was under continual surveillance for the rest of his life, and his work was subject to a double censorship – the normal State censorship and that of the chief of police, Benkendorf. In 1831 Pushkin married Natalia Goncharov, the beautiful daughter of an impoverished Moscow family. The marriage brought little happiness. On 27 January 1837 he was mortally wounded in a duel with a French Guards officer, d'Anthes, who had been carrying on a scandalous flirtation with the poet's wife. Pushkin's death so angered the populace – who suspected the authorities of condoning, if not encouraging, the fatal duel – that in the interests of public security the poet's corpse was smuggled out of the capital in the dead of night, to be carried to Mikhailovskoye for burial.

Such 'brief lives' are always a travesty and never more so than in Pushkin's case. More revealing, really, to quote Push-kin's account of himself, in a letter to a gushing female admirer: 'Perhaps I am elegant and genteel in my writings; but my heart is completely vulgar.' He wrote like an angel, and he felt, enjoyed, suffered, like a coach-driver or a typist. In standing on the common, even commonplace, ground of human experience, he resembled Shakespeare: the poet who, after the youthful influence of Byron had receded, occupied a central role in his creative imagination.

It is ironic that Pushkin – of all major poets the least known outside his own country – was also the most dependent on foreign authors. A native literature hardly existed. The rules of prosody had had to be imported in the mid-eighteenth century, trundled in from Germany like some precious raw material unobtainable in Russia. The aristocracy spoke in French, considering their own tongue barbaric. Pushkin had to create his own tradition. In fifteen years of mature life he virtually founded Russian literature and became its crowning achievement. Even with his towering genius, the achievement would not have been possible had he not steeped himself in western authors. Thanks to his father's library – about the only thing he could thank his parents for – he gained an extensive knowledge of French literature while still only a boy. French, of course, sprang as naturally to his lips as the Russian he heard so richly spoken by his nurse, Arina Rodionovna. For a long time, however, he had to read English writers at second hand, through pallid French translations; yet still he caught, and was excited by, their force and robustness. No wonder he called translators 'the post-horses of enlightenment'. All that he read and heard he transformed into his own uniquely balanced, harmonious style.

As a poet he refuses to be categorized. He is a Romantic in the exuberance of his imagination, and in the strength and directness of his emotional expression; yet above all he is concise and restrained. Rather than ecstasy, he emphasizes the importance of calm as the prerequisite of creation. He writes as joyfully about the pop of champagne corks as about girls' kisses under moonlight. His friends were disappointed with *Eugene Onegin* because it dealt with everyday social life – poets should be above such trivialities. But Pushkin knew better. They also thought the work was satirical; and Pushkin was stung by that misunderstanding, knowing satire to be quite foreign to his nature. Apart from obviously satirical squibs about his enemies, his work does not attack, but observes and celebrates. He was, also, a little wary of 'poetic licence', and did not like to stray too far from the common reality of prose. In the last years of his life, in fact, he wrote more prose than verse. It was not, as some critics claim, that he was running out of inspiration: prose had always appealed to him. Just as he had written a novel in verse, *Eugene Onegin*, so now he wrote poetry in the form of prose novels and short stories. Always his imagination kept moving on, eager for new forms. There is even a late, haunting fragment, *Egyptian*

Nights, in which prose and verse are blended. Like much of his work, it appears to be a century before its time.

That inexhaustibly ranging imagination may be glimpsed, I hope, even through the dark glass of translation. The lyric poems in the first part of the present selection may give a hint – if nothing else – of how he could project his sensibility into the future, like a ghostly peninsula. It is difficult to imagine an English poet of his time writing some of the love poems. Three of them, 'Under the blue skies of her native land . . .', 'For the shores of your distant home . . .' and 'Invocation', are about Amalia Riznich, a merchant's wife with whom he had had a relationship in Odessa. She had fallen ill with tuberculosis, become pregnant, and been 'banished' by her husband to Italy. Pushkin had quickly consoled himself elsewhere. When, two years later, he was told she had died, he was unmoved. Then, his very lack of emotion struck him like a blow to the heart. Naked in their honesty as in their sorrow, the three lyrics to Amalia were written, not all at once but over several years. They reach towards the psychological realism of the twentieth century.

A similar 'naked' love poem was written to his wife: 'No, I don't miss the dissipated nights . . .'. Natalia was beautiful but cold. Though she was, for the most part, dutiful and faithful, she did not love Pushkin. She found his poems boring. Yet, after the scores or hundreds of light conquests and excitable girls, there was excitement and pleasure in her lack of response. His poem expresses it with amazing candour, but also with restraint and tenderness. Another lyric which has the fractured air of a modern poem is 'Lines Written at Night during Insomnia': a brief sequence of fragmentary images, yet adding up to an overwhelming question. In the poems beginning 'A deaf man . . .' and 'My rubicund critic . . .' we find the black or absurd humour we thought an invention of our own age. The first is pure farce; the second

13

lulls us into smiles at the sheer boredom of rural solitude before jolting us with its last terrifying image, the peasant carrying a child's coffin under his arm.

'The Prophet', in contrast, is charged energy. So is 'Demons'. This poem is simultaneously a terrifying evocation of a man and his coach-driver caught in a snowstorm and, in the words of John Bayley, 'a symbolic snowstorm, an obsession endlessly circling in the mind to the point of madness'.[1] Apart from the demons in the poet's own mind, it reaches out across a century to the delirium of 1917 and Blok's 'The Twelve'. Completely different in style and mood is 'I have visited again . . . ', a meditation reminiscent of Wordsworth, tranquilly celebrating the process of ageing, death, and continuance through children and grandchildren. This poem expresses an important but often hidden aspect of Pushkin's vulgar heart. He was 'obedient to life's law'. At a deeper level than the flamboyant expressions of individuality – the eccentric clothes, the grotesquely long fingernails, the pistol practice at his bedroom ceiling – he believed that 'there is no happiness outside the ordinary'. It was this belief, far more than passion, that made him decide to get married. He had grave misgivings: marriage 'castrates the soul', he said, and 'lawful cunt' was like a warm cap into which one's whole head would vanish. But it was time. Time to settle down, to have children. There is an endearing story of Pushkin waking up his small children to show them off proudly to a visitor. His final obedience to life's law was in his request that he should be buried at Mikhailovskoye beside his mother – a woman who had been brittle and trivial, and given him little love.

That final choice also reflects his devotion to the feminine. All his life, the rustle and scent of a woman's dress made him giddy with desire. The sexual and creative instincts in him ran as parallel as the twin blades of a skater. Drawings of women's faces, bosoms and feet decorate the margins of his notebooks;

1. *Pushkin*, Cambridge University Press, 1971, p.63.

14

even when announcing *Boris Godunov*, that most masculine of plays, he promised his friend Vyazemsky: 'Marina will make you get a hard on – because she is a Pole and very good looking . . .'.[1] That's rather like Shakespeare assuring Ben Jonson that Portia in *Julius Caesar* would make him feel randy.

The most surprising image in the ode 'Autumn' – a comparison of the attractions of late autumn with those of a consumptive girl – is therefore not so surprising after all. Autumn was Pushkin's favourite season, the time when he felt healthiest and most creative. So the poem is about the season, but finally about the act of poetic creation. Autumn, the young woman, the verses springing to the pen, the start of the voyage of discovery – enough has been said; and the ode breaks off, in a characteristic Pushkinian way. Described as a fragment, it is one of his most perfect poems.

The selection of longer poems and dramas in this book demonstrates further the amazing diversity of his genius. The first was written when he was only twenty-one, but the style and construction are already mature. It is also extraordinarily imaginative. Pushkin had no time for organized religion; though, not long before his fatal duel, he told a friend that he had come to believe in God – in a vague, mystical way. There is nothing vague or mystical about God in his only 'religious' poem, 'The Gavriliad'. God, surrounded by harp-playing sycophants, moons lovesick over a beautiful young Jewess who has caught his eye down on earth. The girl, Mary, is married to a rather incompetent old carpenter, who 'does not trouble her'. God sends down Gabriel as his go-between. With feminine irrationality, Mary prefers this languid Guards-officer type to the King of Heaven. Satan also takes a hand. Mary, previously immaculate, enjoys Satan, Gabriel and God, all in one day: not to mention a little autoerotic pleasure.

There could be no question of his publishing, or even

1. *Letters*, ed. J. T. Shaw, Wisconsin, 1967, p.261.

acknowledging, so outrageous a piece. Like present-day *samizdat*, copies passed from hand to hand, and the poem enjoyed immense clandestine popularity. Everyone knew it was Pushkin's: so witty, indecent, pure, sexy, charming, engaging – who else could have written it? I can imagine young Pushkin chuckling wildly as the verses flowed, hopping about his room in astonished delight at some idea even more hilariously improper than the last. It is a strongly life-affirming work, in fact; as well as humour there is tenderness in his portrayal of a sixteen-year-old girl coming at last into full possession of her body, entranced by the wonder of her discovery.

Determinedly, all his life, he denied authorship of 'The Gavriliad', though it is likely that he confessed his youthful folly in secret to Tsar Nicholas I. It is a wonder that he got away with it at the time of writing, for he was really playing with fire: to have brought sex into the Christian religion – it was the profoundest blasphemy. Already 'on probation' in southern Russia, he was under constant scrutiny. He went on playing with fire. An affair with the wife of General Vorontsov, his administrative superior and 'guardian', did not endear him to the latter. Vorontsov dispatched his under-secretary of the tenth class to investigate and report on a plague of locusts in the Chersonese. It is said that Pushkin's report was in verse:

> The locusts were flying, flying,
> Then they came to earth,
> They crawled, they ate up everything,
> And then flew off again.

The last straw was a mildly approving reference to atheism, in a letter opened by the police. He was exiled officially to his parents' estate in the north-west, under the strict surveillance of the local police and clergy. In the barrenness of Mikhailovskoye, Pushkin was bored, continued *Eugene Onegin*, immersed himself in Shakespeare, wrote *Boris Godunov*, flirted with a harem of girls at a nearby estate, fell in love with Anna Kern (a visiting cousin at that convenient harem of fluttery maidens), listened to his old nurse's legends, got one of his serf-girls pregnant, longed for Petersburg and his friends, pleaded for release, assured the authorities he was dying of a varicose vein, and wrote and wrote when the mood took him.

Pushkin completed at Mikhailovskoye the last and finest of his Poems of the South, 'The Gypsies'. Its Byronic hero, Aleko, is himself an exile, hunted by the law for some crime left unexplained. Enchanted by the free life of the Bessarabian gypsies, and in particular by the passionate gypsy-girl Zemfira, he joins their wandering band. But his vision of primitive freedom is a fantasy; he cannot endure its reality when he finds it in Zemfira, who tires of him and takes another lover. Aleko kills them both. The gypsies, who have no laws and no executioners, do not punish him but simply turn their faces against him, expelling him from the family.

More clearly of the Romantic era than any of Pushkin's other major works, 'The Gypsies' is often melodramatic in its vocabulary, yet maintains an underlying classical restraint, a tragic decorum. The sombre fatalism of its conclusion ('Everywhere fateful passions swarm/And no one can resist the fates') is no mere conventional formula but a conclusion from the evidence of the poem. It is also in tune with Pushkin's essentially sober mood in the Mikhailovskoye years. The consciousness of hovering fate is deeply present, for example, in '19 October', his poem of friendship and loneliness written in 1825. His departure from the warm south to the bleak northern landscape perhaps marked for the poet the end of his youth, the onset of awareness that he was mortal. Russia was also moving towards a tragic event which would bring disaster perilously close to him; he may have sensed its approaching shadow.

'The Bridegroom', a poem on an altogether smaller scale than 'The Gypsies', is in the form of a popular ballad. Natasha, a merchant's daughter, comes home in a distraught state, after going missing for three days. Her parents fear the worst. Conveniently, the village matchmaker turns up with a proposition they cannot refuse. At the wedding-feast the bride unfolds a 'dream' which explains her terror. Sharp realism, touched by the uncanny, reminds us of Freudian case-studies ('Everything was now clear. The unfortunate young woman . . .'). Pushkin's ballad is all matter-of-factness and compression; the climactic horror is shattering but brief – dissolving almost at once into normality.

'Count Nulin', a major masterpiece, belongs entirely to the sunlit ordinary world, yet there is a touch of the uncanny about its composition. At the end of November, 1825, Pushkin was overjoyed to hear of the death of Alexander I, since he hoped the new Tsar might release him from exile. On 11 December, knowing nothing of the political uncertainty in the capital, he set out recklessly for St Petersburg. On the road he passed two hares and a monk in black, and superstitiously turned back home. Had he gone on, he could scarcely have avoided involvement in the abortive *coup d'état* of 14 December and suffering the fate of his friends: permanent exile in Siberia. Instead, on 12 and 13 December he wrote a joyous comedy set in a remote country house, but with a young housewife – not a poet – as the bored occupant longing for diversion. He may have written the work, as Troyat suggests, 'to occupy his mind and relieve his rattled nerves'.[1] He may have been saved by two hares and a monk. Or did he have 'Nulin' brooding in his mind when he set off, and did his muse gently persuade him to turn back and write it? Every poet knows and likes the person from Porlock who provides a welcome interruption; but sometimes there is that other person, equally likeable, who answers the door first and tells the

1. *Pushkin*, Allen & Unwin, 1974, p.290.

person from Porlock to go away . . . or who provides hares and monks to dissuade the superstitious poet from travelling.

Pushkin's lucky comedy is as real, earthy, clear, as a painting by Breughel. A country house in the wilds, the master gone hunting, a bored mistress, and the joy of a surprise guest: a coach has overturned on the road. The slightly injured fop, Count Nulin, is unexpectedly charmed by his rustic hostess, makes a pass at her, and is repulsed. Nothing more. Yet the house and muddy yard, the lively young wife Natasha, the absurd Count, the sly servant Parasha, live forever. 'Nothing even in *Evgeny Onegin*,' observes John Bayley, 'is so electrically charged with life as the beginning of "Count Nulin".'[1] And the electric charge keeps running. The poem was conceived as a parody of Shakespeare's *The Rape of Lucrece*. What would have happened, Pushkin wondered, if Lucrece had simply slapped Tarquin's face? But the parodic intention vanished in the making. If any Shakespearean influence remains, it is to be found in the vivid characterization and the dramatic gusto of the five 'scenes' – the departure of the hunt, the Count's arrival, the evening's flirtation, the attempted seduction, the master's return at breakfast-time: from the plays rather than from the languid narrative poem. But it is all Pushkin's own. A day and a night in the country. Phrases of time keep recurring: 'It's time,' 'meantime', 'late', and so on. Simple chronological time, not 'the hour is at hand' or anything apocalyptic. An ordinary house, an ordinary young woman. The truth of it, the delight of it. Life's plenty.

And it is achieved with an almost total absence of figurative language. Always sparing with metaphors and similes, Pushkin here outdoes himself. The literalness is deliberate; it is actually an incredible technical feat to write so long a work virtually without metaphor and simile, and to achieve a glowing, life-filled canvas. Beneath the surface there is a suggestion of balanced forces: the life of the seasons outside,

1. *Pushkin*, op. cit., p.292.

the life of the house; the hunt for animals, the hunt for another kind of prey; the master's sleeping rough, the visitor's search for the soft fleece; the master's hunting-gear, the visitor's bedside paraphernalia; the Count's artifice beside Natasha's naturalness. There is also an intricate dance of sexual intrigues, the drollest of which is kept till the very end. In its balancing of energies and emblems, 'Count Nulin' is reminiscent of the medieval English poem *Sir Gawain and the Green Knight*. In the Russian poem, the subtle and serious harmonies are wholly subordinate to realism and humour.

It is generally agreed that Pushkin's greatest achievement in pure dramatic form was not *Boris Godunov* but his *Little Tragedies*, highly compressed psychological dramas. 'Mozart and Salieri' and 'The Stone Guest' were written in the autumn of 1830, at Boldino in Nizhny Novgorod. The Boldino estate was an engagement gift from his parents and Pushkin had gone to look over his property. An outbreak of cholera around Moscow kept him there for three months. Isolated from social distractions, including his bride-to-be Natalia Goncharov, he made rich creative use of his tedium. Poised uncertainly on the verge of domestic responsibilities, his mind must have been whirling between arrivals and departures, as though at one of those railway stations that haunt Russian literature. The Pushkin who would leave Boldino for Petersburg and Natalia would be a stranger. This dividing of the ways within himself may have contributed to his choice of subjects: Mozart, the creator and Don Juan, the lover, both on the verge of death. For in renouncing his freedom, Pushkin feared that both the lover in him and the creator were at risk.

'Mozart and Salieri' is based on the legend that the latter poisoned Mozart out of envy. Pushkin gives to Salieri a nobler and more interesting motive. He loves Mozart the man, and is moved to tears of joy by his music – but the genius does not take art seriously enough. He has nothing to say, nothing to contribute, except through his compositions, which are so immeasurably superior to the works of other composers that they can produce only discouragement. Mozart's offensive frivolity, or appearance of frivolity, resembles that of the poet Charsky in Pushkin's unfinished story, *Egyptian Nights*: 'He avoided the society of his literary brothers, preferring men of the world, even the most simple-minded, to their company. His conversation was extremely commonplace and never touched on literature.' Secretly, however, Charsky was only happy when inspiration possessed him, when he experienced what he called his 'silly season'. Then he wrote in a passion; and there was nothing more to be said. How frustrating for the serious, talented creators, like Salieri, who never tire of theorizing. Art must be saved from its disreputable geniuses. Salieri drops the poison in Mozart's cup.

Disreputable Pushkin kept a list of the women he had loved. Just as in his art he moved obsessively from one work to another, totally possessed for a season and then regarding the finished products 'as nothing but merchandise at so much per piece', so – until Natalia – he had moved from woman to woman. Now it was going to stop. His situation can be glimpsed in 'The Stone Guest'. Don Juan finds his greatest triumph and his nemesis at the same instant. His triumph is to persuade a grieving and virtuous widow, Donna Anna, to grant him 'one cold, quiet' kiss, after revealing himself as the slayer of her husband, the Commander. But Donna Anna is not like all the other women; there is a quality about her, a stillness of soul, that unnerves him. And outside her house the Commander's marble statue, drawn from the cemetery at the Don's bidding to stand guard over his *amours*, awaits his exit. He crushes Juan's hand in his heavy fist – rather like a father congratulating a future son-in-law . . . Is this, at last, *love* that Don Juan is feeling? Does he love the statuesque Donna Anna as Pushkin loved Natalia Goncharov? If so, it is very like death.

All Juan's previous affairs, including his cheerful and com-
radely relationship with the actress Laura, have been a kind of
coitus interruptus, allowing him freedom to move on to another.
But the passion he feels, or thinks he feels, for Donna Anna
contains finality. The last line of the drama is consummation
and death: 'I'm perishing – all's over – O Donna Anna!'

Or perhaps his love for Donna Anna is still only a pretence.
'Who knows? Who knows you?' as she says to him. 'The Stone
Guest' leaves the question unanswered. 'We're our own
masters,' Leporello observes. We may guess what Juan is
thinking, but we don't *know*, any more than Laura knows – or
cares – what the weather is like, far away in Paris. Pushkin's
characters retain their inner freedom. Clear and mysterious as
great art is, 'The Stone Guest' has exercised an enduring
fascination over later Russian poets; the Commander's stone
steps echo again in Blok and Akhmatova.

'Rusalka', the other drama in this selection, can also find
echoes in Pushkin's life. At Mikhailovskoye in 1826 he got a
serf-girl, Olga Kalashnikova, with child. He made kindly,
businesslike arrangements for her; she was married and later
lived in Boldino. In the year of that troublesome event,
Pushkin made the first sketches for 'Rusalka', though he did
not take up the work again until 1832. The legends of the
northern Slavs depict rusalkas as malignant river-nymphs
who lure humans into the water to drown them. Often they
are girls who have drowned themselves for love, and seek
revenge. That is what happens in Pushkin's version: a miller's
daughter is seduced by a prince; when he abandons her to
marry someone more suitable, buying her off with gifts, she
throws herself into the Dnieper, with their unborn child. But
the prince is haunted by her, and finds no happiness in his
marriage. He is drawn back to the river-bank where he had
been happier than he knew. The drama breaks off at the point
at which a *rusalochka* – his unknown daughter – appears before
him, sent by her mother to lure him into the river.

The relationship between life and art being an extremely subtle one, it is of course dangerous to read personal factors into a work of literature. And in Pushkin's case particularly, whatever personal turbulence may or may not exist in the depths, the surface – the poem itself – is radiantly clear and without secrets. Yet I think we can divine, in the origins of 'Rusalka', that conscience of the poet which observed compassionately and remorsefully the plight of women with whom his Don Juan self had trifled. He is on their side – against Pushkin. It is a feature that links 'Rusalka' with 'The Stone Guest', *Eugene Onegin*, and such lyrics as 'Under the blue skies of her native land . . .', 'Do not sing to me again . . .', and even, in a different way, 'To my Nanny'. There is in all his writings a profound understanding of, and empathy with, women; and nowhere is it more evident than in 'Rusalka'. The passionate warmth of the miller's daughter changes, after her transformation, only to a passionate coldness. And Pushkin understands that this kind of passion can cast an even greater seductive spell on its victim. The terseness, psychological truth and dramatic power of 'Rusalka' are equally wonderful. Though it is formally incomplete, it is as finished and perfect as that other 'fragment', 'Autumn'. One can imagine no conclusion more chillingly effective than the brief wordless appearance on the river-bank of the *rusalochka*, the prince's unborn daughter.

While the influence of Slavic folk-tales is obvious in 'Rusalka', it is often a difficult, as well as an unproductive, task to identify Pushkin's sources. His old nurse, Arina Rodionovna, is credited with providing him with the oral 'book of the people'; yet the stories she told him had sometimes filtered through to her from modern literature. Like all great writers, Pushkin cared not a whit where or what he scavenged. His *skazka*, or fairy-tale, 'The Golden Cockerel' actually owes as much to a story by Washington Irving, which he had read in a

French translation, as it does to the native oral tradition. The poet blends, in this tale as in 'Tsar Saltan', an atmosphere of primitive magic and naivety with a sharp modern realism. The warlike, despotic Tsar Dadon, who belatedly wants peace and quiet in his old age, may be in part an ironic backward glance at Alexander I; but any political significance is perfectly disguised by childlike enchantment. At the same time the fairy-tale enchantment never stops us from feeling a prickle of reality. 'The Golden Cockerel' is closer in spirit to Ibsen's *The Master Builder* than to Tolkien's *The Hobbit*.

And 'The Tale of Tsar Saltan' seems to me closer to Shakespeare's late romances than to any of our English fantasies; though, of course, its seriousness is of quite a different kind from Shakespeare's – the seriousness of pure beauty and perfect, exuberant narrative. It gives delight and hurts not. 'Tsar Saltan' is, as John Bayley says, 'a triumph of simple tale-telling, which has no equivalent in European verse – only in the prose of Grimm and Hans Andersen'. There are magical island-kingdoms, and lost heirs, and three witches, and a swan-princess; yet this enchanted world is in touch with real emotion: the magical characters have human nature. To quote one scarcely noticeable example: the lost heir, Duke Guidon, rushes his wedding-day just like his father before him – he has inherited impatience! More importantly, when the swan-princess tells the Duke that his destiny is not far away but close at hand, and when the old Tsar recognizes his long-lost wife and son, truth and magic combine as surely as they do on Prospero's island.

D. S. Mirsky, in his *History of Russian Literature*, goes so far as to say that 'the longer one lives, the more one is inclined to regard "Tsar Saltan" as the masterpiece of Russian poetry'. Yet the Himalayas of Pushkin's art also includes such peaks as *Eugene Onegin*, 'The Stone Guest', 'Count Nulin' and 'Rusalka', and it is very hard to decide which overtops all others. Each one seems the highest when one is climbing it. Yet if one must find the Everest, probably it is 'The Bronze Horseman'. Written during the poet's second and last visit to Boldino, this poem encompasses the essential story of the next century and a half: the hapless struggle of the individual to survive, in an increasingly estranged urban environment, against absolute power – whether of emperor or ideology. There are three 'personages' in the poem: Falconet's bronze equestrian statue of Peter the Great, monument to the iron will that built a city on water at enormous cost in human suffering; the Neva, which burst its banks in November 1824, flooding Petersburg; and – the only living person – Yevgeni, a humble clerk, whose one ambition is to marry the girl he loves and live an ordinary family life. The flood destroys his modest dream; driven mad, he wanders the streets like a tramp and whenever he comes across the bronze statue he grows agitated, doffs his cap to the 'Idol', and quickly moves on.

Admiration for the stern beauty of Petersburg and for its maker coexists in 'The Bronze Horseman' with compassion for the ordinary people, like Yevgeni, who are swept aside as of no account. Style and content are perfectly matched; when Yevgeni enters the scene the verses become pale, flat, deliberately close to cliché; but when the Horseman enters they take on a metallic clangor. Tsar Nicholas did not like the portrayal of his predecessor. He insisted that all references to the 'Idol' should be removed, as well as the crucial episode in which Yevgeni imagines himself pursued by the statue through the streets. Rather than permit such cuts, Pushkin declined to publish. The poem first appeared, in a bowdlerized form, after his death.

When Solzhenitsyn paused under the statue of Pushkin and promised not to stray from the true path, he must have called to mind the poor madman pausing under that other statue. He may also have found strength in the knowledge that Pushkin had outlasted the tyrants. In the words of Blok: 'There are the solemn names of emperors, generals, inventors

112,434

LIBRARY
College of St. Francis
JOLIET, ILL.

of instruments of death, torturers and martyrs; and alongside them this one bright sound: Pushkin.'

2

Translating Pushkin

In the half-century following Pushkin's death, a dozen versions of his prose tales, *The Captain's Daughter* and *The Queen of Spades*, were published in Britain and America. Of the verse there was next to nothing. Matthew Arnold in his essay on Tolstoy remarked that the crown of literature was poetry, and the Russians had not yet had a great poet. John Greenleaf Whittier thought that Russia's best poet, a man called Pushkin, was a negro.[1] The twentieth century has not lacked translations of the poems,[2] but the mediocre quality of most of them has led English readers to conclude either that Pushkin is overrated by his fellow countrymen or that he is untranslatable. The most obvious reason for the mediocrity is that the Russian language has rarely been understood by English-speaking poets. Poets should always be translated by poets. In Russia, Shakespeare has had the good fortune to be translated by Pasternak.

There are, naturally, many problems for the translator that spring from the very nature of Russian. It is a conservative language, retaining an inflected syntax. This offers to the poet enormous scope for varying the word-order, thereby adjusting the emotional stress; and the echoing harmonies of the case-endings create an enviable richness of sound. To glimpse even a shadow of the former we have to turn to the more flexible word-order of Shakespearean English: 'How oft when

1. He was actually the great-grandson of an Abyssinian, on his mother's side.
2. But the range is somewhat narrow: very few versions of 'Count Nulin', 'The Stone Guest' and 'Rusalka', for instance.

thou, my music, music play'st . . .'. The Russian language seems closer to the childhood of symbolic expression; it can grunt, groan, sigh, laugh and weep with a marvellous, truthful naivety – as when Tatiana, in *Eugene Onegin*, *to vzdókhnyet*, *to ókhnyet*, 'now sighs, now oh's'. The *shum* and *khókhot* of her name-day party seem closer to the actual fleshly reality than are 'bustle and laughter'. No English horse gallops like Peter the Great's in 'The Bronze Horseman': *kak budto gróma grokhotánye*, 'like a roar of thunder'. An English girl's amorous trembling cannot match a Russian girl's *tryepyetánye*. Moreover, her 'little feet', so often found in English translations, sound pallid and Little Nell-ish; whereas the *nózhki* so beloved by Pushkin suggests in Russian something like 'slender adorable erotic little feet'. Russia's infinitely various diminutives trip us up.

Yet Russian and English share a rich vocabulary, strong rhythms, a related prosody. I can't believe it is harder to translate from Russian than from the language whose Biblical equivalent of 'Thy rod and Thy staff' is *ton baton*.

Admittedly, Pushkin is especially difficult. While he exploits to the utmost all the primitive sophistication of his native tongue, he gives the impression of being totally simple. His most moving lines are often so simple that we do not know why we are moved. As examples of this quality, Maurice Baring and John Bayley respectively quote lines from 'The Covetous Knight' and 'Rusalka':

> *I mórye, gdye byezháli korablí . . .*
> [And the sea, where ships were running . . .]

> *Ostáls'a*
> *Odín v'lyesú na byéryegu Dnyeprá.*
> [He has stayed
> Alone in the forest on the Dnieper's bank.]

One of his favourite words is *tíkho*, 'quietly'. His muse, he said, was a simple country girl.

Pasternak, through Doctor Zhivago's Varykino diary, says this of Pushkin's art: 'Concrete things – things in the outside world, things in current use, names of things, common nouns – burst in and take possession of his verse, driving out the vaguer parts of speech.' Faced with the problem that these concrete nouns and verbs are usually longer, more polysyllabic, than their English counterparts, translators are tempted to fill out a line with those vaguer parts of speech; so that, for instance, 'much in my life has changed' becomes 'and many things/Have altered in the life that wraps me round'; 'it's ruined' becomes 'It's fall'n into disuse, a heap of ruins'; and so on. Such travesties are commonplace – and fatal for a poet who, in his best work, makes every word count. It is far better to make the English version shorter, or to create some bold invention that stays true to Pushkin's lively and concrete style.

Another difficulty is his avoidance of metaphor, the aspect of poetry that translates better than any other. With a few brilliant exceptions, he is content with brief and traditional comparisons, such as stars, storm, shadow, dream, the moon. His poetry withdraws into the bare structure of the language, ignoring those elements which transcend linguistic boundaries. To achieve a comparable effect in English we may sometimes have to invent a metaphor. This is perilous; but timidity rather than daring is more often the curse of translations.

Like a husband who makes love to his wife while fantasizing another, an apparently faithful translation can be insidiously astray. Together with 'I loved you . . .', the most frequently translated of all Pushkin's poems is the lyric 'To Anna Kern'. Anna Kern was the beautiful wife of a senile general. Pushkin met her in a Petersburg salon in 1819, sought a liaison and was rebuffed. In 1825 he met her again when she visited her relations near Mikhailovskoye, fell passionately in love with her and wrote his poem. Briefly they became lovers, when the edge of his passion was already blunted. And thereafter they became firm friends. Here is the first verse of the lyric, with some English versions:

> *Ya pómnyu chúdnoye mgnovyénye:*
> [I remember the wonderful moment:]
> *Pyeryedo mnóy yavílas tý,*
> [Before me/didst appear/thou,]
> *Kak mimolyótnoye vidyénye,*
> [Like a fleeting apparition,]
> *Kak gyéniy chístoy krasotý.*
> [Like a genius of pure beauty.]

> A moment I recall entrancing;
> Before my eyes thy form arose,
> A fleeting vision past me glancing,
> Where beauty's self serenely glows.
>
> Sir Cecil Kisch[1]

> I mind me still of that strange meeting
> When thou didst pass before my sight –
> A momentary vision fleeting,
> A spirit pure and blest and bright.
>
> Rosa Newmarch[2]

> Yes, I remember well our meeting,
> When first thou dawnedst on my sight,

---

1. *The Wagon of Life*, Cresset Press, 1947.
2. *Poetry and Progress in Russia*, Bodley Head, 1907.

Like some fair phantom past me fleeting,
Some nymph of purity and light.

Thomas B. Shaw[1]

I call to mind a moment's glory.
You stood before me, face to face,
Like to a vision transitory,
A spirit of immaculate grace.

C. M. Bowra[2]

All four versions seem faithful enough, keeping close to the meaning and the form. Or so it appears, from a surface glance. Really, they are utterly remote from Pushkin. 'To Anna Kern' is one of the hardest of all his lyrics to translate; I can only justify my criticism of these honourable attempts because I know my own version also fails, in a different way.

Bowra is right to reject *thou*, since it is (sadly for poetry) archaic in English though normal usage in Russian. 'Call to mind' is not the same as 'remember', and 'moment's glory' strikes a more artificial note than the original; 'like to' is strained, as is the inversion of 'vision transitory'. His last line is too other-worldly, too like Wordsworth's 'phantom of delight'. Pushkin's 'genius of pure beauty' is not, despite appearances, so completely a denial of his later and coarser view, as expressed in a letter to a friend: 'You don't write me anything about the 2,100 roubles I owe you, but you write me about Madame Kern, whom, with God's help, a few days ago I fucked.' Bowra has produced a polished verse, as we might expect from so fine a scholar – only it is not Pushkin.

An English tutor at the Tsarskoye Selo *lycée*, Thomas Shaw deserves respect for writing the first authentic account in a

1. *Blackwood's Magazine*, 1845.
2. *A Book of Russian Verse*, Macmillan, 1943.

British journal of Pushkin's life; and he also offered several translations. His version of the stanza is manly and dignified, but too brisk. His first line suggests a cheerful chance encounter. Rosa Newmarch's 'mind me' is awkward, and her 'strange meeting' (pre-Wilfred Owen) is inaccurate: wonder, not strangeness, is being expressed. Kisch's 'entrancing', especially so crudely misplaced, is clearly only there for the rhyme – but there is no sign either that Mrs Kern was glancing past Pushkin or, for that matter, glowing. Yet in his foreword to Sir Cecil Kisch's translations, Bowra complimented him on keeping 'as closely as possible to the meaning and metre of the original text'.

As far as meaning is concerned in our exemplary stanza, Kisch only *looks* close, in the way that Leningrad looks close to Moscow on a world map. Such apparent, superficial closeness can too easily cover a yawning chasm. Metrically, too, his version is both close and distant. That is, he uses the iambic tetrameter, like Pushkin; but if there were scales to weigh verses, Kisch's would be several grams heavier. This is through no fault of his – the nature of the Russian language allows their tetrameters to run more lightly and elegantly than ours.[1] This is an important difference, since the iambic tetrameter was Pushkin's favourite form: almost half of his poetry is in this metre. It came as naturally to him as blank verse to Shakespeare. Metres change when they cross frontiers, and translators have to take account of that. It may well be, in most cases, that the 'same' metre will be the most appropriate; but it is not self-evident, and there will be exceptions.

---

1. There are often only two or three words in a Russian tetrameter, because of their polysyllabic vocabulary, and even the longest word carries only one stress: *Kak mimolyótnoye vidyénye*. Moreover, a stress can never be displaced into a 'weak' position – a common feature in English verse: 'On the báld stréet brèaks the blánk dáy'. The effect of Tennyson's line is impossible to achieve in Russian, and the effect of Pushkin's equally so in English.

The 'same' rhyme-scheme is also different. Russians have an abundance of rhymes, both masculine and feminine. We are poorer in this resource, especially in feminine rhymes. Pushkin commonly alternates masculine and feminine rhymes, with perfect naturalness; but if an English translator tries to emulate him, his rhymes are bound to be more obvious and strained. 'Entrancing' and 'glancing', 'meeting' and 'fleeting' – hardly the art which conceals art. 'Fidelity' to Pushkin's rhymes courts disaster, especially when it has to be sustained over several hundred lines, as in 'Count Nulin', 'The Gypsies' or 'The Bronze Horseman'. A greater faithfulness will usually be achieved by subduing the rhyme in some way. There are, of course, a few works where the advantages of keeping the full masculine–feminine alternation outweigh the disadvantages. *Eugene Onegin* is the classic example – though it needed Charles Johnston's technical virtuosity and poetic tact to bring it off. In this present selection, I decided that 'Demons' and 'Winter Road' were exceptional cases, where the price of straining for feminine rhymes was worth paying.

Generally, however, I have tried to keep faith with the spirit of the poems – and, as far as possible, with their sense – rather than with the poet's Russian apparatus of metres and rhymes. I sought, in each case, an appropriate English form to carry the spirit of the original in (I hoped) a living English poem. The raw edge of emotion in several of the love poems led me away from strict form towards free verse. 'I loved you . . .', in contrast, has a formal elegance, rather like a Caroline lyric, which made me want to stay close to Pushkin's rhyming pentameter. 'Autumn', originally in hexameters, moved naturally into English pentameter, irregularly rhymed.

Each of the long poems and dramas also presented a unique problem. 'Count Nulin', 'Tsar Saltan' and 'The Golden Cockerel' are in tetrameters in the original; and they moved readily enough into English tetrameter, which is admirably suited to gaiety and humour. 'The Gypsies' and 'The Bronze Horseman' resisted such a transition. Or rather, in the case of the former, it seemed to want the four-stress line but to refuse rhyme altogether. The unrhymed tetrameter is an awkward and rare form in English, but it was the best that could be done – an extremely loose version of tetrameters, verging on free verse. The absence of even a subdued rhyme is a grievous loss; but I have been grieved even more by some assiduously rhymed versions, which inevitably distort the sense and feeling of the original. In 'The Gypsies', the literal sense seems of paramount importance.[1]

That applies even more strongly to 'The Bronze Horseman'. Unlike the humorous poems where a few liberties can be taken, Pushkin's late masterpiece seemed to demand a literal fidelity in every line, but that would be impossible in rhyming tetrameters. Eventually the poem moved into blank verse, allowing me to keep very close to the sense. It struck me also as fitting that, for this central work of Russian literature, our natural and national English metre, blank verse, should replace Russia's, the rhymed tetrameter.

Likewise blank verse appeared to work better for 'The Gavriliad' than the rhymed pentameter of the Russian; and it throws up mock-heroic echoes of Milton. Where Pushkin himself used blank verse, in the dramas, the ghost of Shakespeare stands at the translator's shoulder – a worrying presence, because it is so easy to produce sub-Shakespearean dialogue. Nevertheless, I have used blank verse for 'Rusalka' and 'Mozart and Salieri', though departing from it in Salieri's speeches. For some reason our Elizabethan ghost was more disturbing in 'The Stone Guest'; so I decided to take advantage of this drama's somewhat operatic, larger-than-

1. A section of about forty lines resisted *any* attempt to translate it adequately. Since it is not a crucial passage, I decided to leave it out altogether.

life atmosphere by (ironically) *adding* some irregular rhyme.

What I have tried *not* to do is to dress up Pushkin's simple country girl in flounces. His allegiance was to reality and commonsense. 'His verse always fully mirrored his actual state of mind,' wrote Nadezhda Mandelstam, '– he never posed or invented non-existent situations.' When his Byronic poem 'The Prisoner of the Caucasus' was published, he was exasperated by a critical rebuke for allowing a traveller to sleep in his wet *burka* (a Circassian overcoat) rather than remove it and dry off. '*Burkas* are rainproof,' Pushkin pointed out, 'and only get wet on the outside. Therefore it is possible to sleep in one if you have nothing else to wear, and absolutely pointless to dry it out.' A government censor enraged him by insisting, in the interest of morality, that *nights* be replaced by *days* in the lines, 'Fate gave to him/Few exquisite nights.' 'The censor has butchered me. I will not, must not, cannot say "days" in that line. *Nights, nights*, for the love of Christ, *few exquisite nights*. It has to be nights, because she couldn't come to him in the day. Look at the poem. And why is night more improper than day? Which is the hour of the twenty-four that so offends the sensibility of our censor?'

So, a translator may change anything – but never night into day. Which in Pushkin's case means, above all, retaining some of that 'peace and freedom' so dear to him, not chaining the poem down with too tight a control. In words particularly relevant to Pushkin, Marina Tsvetaeva observes: 'A poet is the reverse of a chess-player. Not only does he not see the pieces and the board, he doesn't even see his own hand – which perhaps is not there.' Translators, too, should not be over-conscious of the board and their hand. Night is also turned into day if, as too many translators have done with Pushkin, they chase the chimera of the 'same' metre and rhyme-scheme while neglecting what is far more important, his rhythm, which is the natural rhythm of human speech. 'Listen to the speech of the people,' he advised. That speech, in all its emotional shades, is in his poetry. Whatever I have had to give up – and the losses are incalculable – I have tried to keep an echo of Pushkin's living speech, 'the sound of sense'.

Beyond all questions of technique, a translator needs luck and love. Of the former, nothing can be said; and of the latter, nothing needs to be said, I hope. For without love, no one would be so foolish as to try to translate a poet who, as his countrymen have always known, stands with Dante and Shakespeare.

D.M.T.

I · Shorter Poems

TO OLGA MASSON

OLGA, you morning-star,
  Godchild of Aphrodite,
Miracle of beauty,
How accustomed you are
To sting with a caress,
With insults to stir
Frenzy. You fix the hour
Of secret voluptuousness
With a hot kiss; then
When all on fire we come,
We stand outside
And hear you whispering
To your grumbling maid;
Your mocking laugh;
The door stays barred.

For the sake of our love
And priapic folly,
For the sake of abandonment,
Of gold, of your charms,
Olga, priestess of lust,
We beg you – appoint for us
Without fail one night
Of rapture, of oblivion.

[1819]

TO THE SEA

FAREWELL, free element!
Before me for the last time
Your blue waves roll
And you shine in proud beauty.

Like a friend's dying words,
His cry in the last hour,
I have heard for the last time
Your moan, your cry, your lament.

My soul's yearned-for home,
How often on your shores
I have wandered, gloomy, quiet,
Tormented by wild thoughts!

How I love your echoes, your dim
Whispering boom, the voice
Of the deep, the evening calm,
And your capricious blasts!

By some whim you choose
To cherish the fisherman's
Humble sail, and it scuds bravely;
But suddenly you grow moody
And devour a whole fleet.

Something has held me back
From quitting forever
The safety of your shore,
From sailing out with rapture
And poetic flight!

You waited, called . . . I was chained down;
My soul struggled for freedom,
In vain; I stayed on your banks
As if a spell was cast around me . . .

Yet where could I have gone?
What is there to regret?
One isle alone in all your wilderness
Might still move my soul:

One cliff, the sepulchre of glory . . .
There, majestic memories subsided
Into chill sleep; the flame
Of Napoleon went out.

And following in his wake,
Like the roar of thunder after lightning,
Another genius fled from us,
Another emperor of the mind.

Byron vanished, mourned by freedom,
Leaving us his garland.
Rage, ocean, tempest-stirred,
At the death of your singer.

Your image was stamped on him,
He was created by your spirit.
Like you, he was powerful, gloomy, deep;
Like you, nothing could daunt him.

The world has grown empty . . . Where
Could you now carry me, O sea?
Enlightenment or tyranny
Have the same iron grip
Wherever virtue quickens.

Farewell, then. I shall not forget
Your triumphant beauty, and long,
Long I shall hear your thunder
In the evening hours.

I shall bear, into the forests
And silent wildernesses, your crags
And creeks, and the glitter and shadow
And murmur of your waves.

[1824]

O rose maiden, you fetter me;
But I am no more ashamed
To be fettered by you
Than is the nightingale, king
Of woodland singers, ashamed
To live close-bound to the rose,
Tenderly singing songs for her
In the obscure voluptuous night.

[1824]

TO THE FOUNTAIN OF THE PALACE
OF
BAKHCHISARAI

Fountain of love, you living source,
Two roses as a gift I bring.
Dear to me is your murmuring voice
That never fails, your tears that spring

Poetically. With light cool rain
Your silver dust is sprinkling me.
Tell me your tale; enchantingly,
Joyously, babble! Pour on, pour on . . .

Fountain of grief, fountain of love!
Questioning your marble I have heard
Praise of a distant land; but of
Maria you say not a word . . .

O, can it be that even here
You are forgotten? The harem's
Glory? . . . And Zarema? Were
You both no more than happy dreams?

In the abyss of fantasy
And the blank dark, did I unfurl
The pale star of Bakhchisarai,
The vague ideal of my soul?

[1824]

As soon as roses fade,
Breathing ambrosia,
Their souls are flying
Lightly to Elysium.

There, where tired waves
Are bearing oblivion,
Their fragrant shades
Bloom over Lethe.

[1825]

TO ANNA KERN

I remember the moment of wonder:
You appeared before me,
Like a momentary vision,
A spirit of pure beauty.

In the oppression of hopeless grief,
In the noisy aimless struggle,
Long I heard your tender voice,
Saw in my dreams your face.

But the years passed. The dreams
Were scattered by turbulent gusts,
And I forgot your tender voice,
Your heavenly face.

In the shadows of seclusion
Quietly my days dragged on,
Without faith and without inspiration,
Without tears, or life, or love.

In my soul, awakening trembled:
And you appeared again,
Like a momentary vision,
A spirit of pure beauty.

And my heart beats in ecstasy,
All that was buried is reborn;
Faith springs again, and inspiration,
And life, and tears, and love.

[1825]

19 OCTOBER

THE woods have cast their crimson foliage,
   The faded field is silvery with frost;
The sun no sooner glimmers than it's lost
Behind drab hills; the world's a hermitage.
Burn brightly, pine-logs, in my lonely cell;
And you, wine, friend to chilly autumn days,
Pour into me a comfortable haze,
Brief respite from the torments of my soul.

Perhaps some friend is driving up by stealth,
Hoping to surprise me; his face will press
Against my window; I'll rush out, embrace
Him warmly, from the heart, then drink his health
And talk, and laugh away our separation
Till dawn. I drink alone; no one will come;
The friends who crowd around me in this room
Are phantoms born of my imagination.

I drink alone, while on the Neva's banks
My comrades speak my name, propose a toast . . .
And who besides myself has missed the feast?
Are there not other spaces in your ranks?
Who else betrays the ritual gathering?
Who has been snatched away by the cold world?
Whose voice is silent when the roll is called?
Who has not come? Who's absent from the ring?

Our curly-headed songster is not there,
With his sweet-tuned guitar and blazing eyes;
Beneath fair myrtles and Italian skies
He calmly sleeps; and on his sepulchre
No friendly chisel has cut out a verse

In Russian, which some stranger in exile
Who wanders there might see, and pause awhile
To mourn a fellow-countryman's resting-place.

And are you seated at the gathering,
Horizon-seeker, you unresting soul,
Or are you off again, for the north pole
And the hot tropics? Pleasant voyaging!
I'm envious of you! Ever since you strode
Out of the school-gates, smiling, and leapt on
The first convenient ship, you've been the son
Of waves and storms, the sea has been your road.

Yet in your wanderings you have faithfully
Preserved the spirit of our boyhood years:
Amid the gales still echoed in your ears
The shouts and merriment of Tsarskoye;
You stretch a hand to us, we know we ride
Safe in your heart wherever you may sail;
And I recall your words: ' It's possible
Our fate is to be scattered far and wide!'

How excellent our union is, how rare!
Beating with one pulse still, as when we first
Linked fast in love, by friendly muses nursed;
In perfect freedom, perfectly secure.
Wherever fate decrees that we must go,
Wherever fortune leads us by the hand,
We're still the same: the world a foreign land,
Our mother country – Tsarskoye Selo.

From place to place driven by the storm, and caught
In nets of a harsh fate, I sought to rest
My weary head upon new friendship's breast,
And trembled when I found what I had sought.

48

But I deceived myself; for though I gave
My heart with all the ardency of youth,
Bitterly I found that trust, and truth,
Were far away in Petersburg, or the grave.

And then, here in this haunt of freezing winds
And blizzards, hope renewed itself, I found
Green shoots emerging from the stony ground;
A brief, sweet solace. Three of you, dear friends,
I embraced here! I could not speak for joy
When you, first, Pushchin, called on me, and chased
Away the dismal thoughts of a disgraced
Poet, as once you cheered a lonely boy.

And you, whom fortune always blessed, I greet you,
Dear Gorchakov! The frigid glare of fame
Has not impaired your heart; you are the same
Free spirit, loyal to your friends and virtue.
Widely divergent are the paths we trace;
Life early separated us; and yet,
When on a country road by chance we met,
There was a brother's warmth in your embrace.

When I was envious even of the shades
Who share my house, since every face had turned
Against me, even my family, I yearned
For you, enchanter of Permessian maids,
My Delvig – and you came, amazingly!
You child of inspired indolence, your voice
Re-kindled fires and made my heart rejoice
At the benevolence of my destiny.

The spirit of song was present in us both,
We shared its agitation and delight
When we were young; two muses paused in flight

And lit on us, nursing each tender growth.
But I grew greedy for applause; your pride
Made you sing for the muses and your soul;
I squandered my whole life, a prodigal;
In quietness your talents multiplied.

The muses won't allow frivolity,
To serve the beautiful one must be sober.
But April's whisper is not like October,
Worldly desires work on us devilishly . . .
We try to call a halt – but it's too late!
We turn round, try to find our lost tracks through
The snow, but can't. That's how it was with you
And I, Wilhelm, my brother in art and fate!

It's time, it's time! The world's not worth the fret
Of all that hunting fever: come, Wilhelm,
Join me here where that fever can grow calm
In solitude. I wait for you; you're late –
Brighten my embers, let our discourse move
Like dawn across those wild Caucasian heights
You and I knew; and where a thought alights
Let's muse awhile – on Schiller, fame, or love.

For me, too, it is time . . . My friends, feast well!
I will imagine mirth and revelry;
Moreover, here's a poet's prophecy:
One more swift year and I'll accept your call;
Everything I want will come to pass;
The months speed by – I'm at your celebrations!
How many tears! How many exclamations!
And lifted high, how many a brimming glass!

And first let's drink to us, our sparkling throng!
And when we've drunk, let's fill our glasses full

Once more, and drink a blessing on our school:
Bless it, triumphant muse – may it live long!
The teachers of that youthful brotherhood,
The dead, the living, we will honour them,
Pressing our grateful lips to the cool rim,
Recall no wrongs, but praise all that was good.

More wine, up to the brim! Our hearts on fire
For the next toast, let's raise the crimson glass!
Whom do we honour now? – but can't you guess?
That's right! Long live the Tsar! We toast the Tsar.
He is a man; confusions, passions, sway
His life like everyone's; he is the slave
Of the passing moment . . . So, his crimes forgive:
He captured Paris, founded our Lycée.

Let us enjoy the feast while we are here!
Alas, our band has dwindled; one is sealed
In the black grave, one's wandering in far fields;
Fate glances, drops her gaze . . . we disappear;
The days flash by, in one year we have grown
Unnoticeably closer to our end . . .
Which one of us, in his old age, my friends,
Will celebrate the founding day alone?

Sad guest of those who will not understand
His tedious words, who barely suffer him,
He will recall us and, his eyes grown dim,
To heavy lids will lift a trembling hand . . .
May he, too, find a poignant consolation
And drink to our friendship in a cup of wine,
As now, in this disgraced retreat of mine,
I've drowned my sadness in your celebration.

[1825]

51

UNDER the blue skies of her native land
   She languished and began to fade . . .
Until – surely – there flew without a sound
   Above me, her young shade;
But there stretches between us an uncrossable line.
   In vain my feelings I tried to awaken.
The lips that brought the news were made of stone,
   And I listened like a stone, unshaken.
So this is she for whom my soul once burned
   In the tense and heavy fire,
Obsessed, exhausted, driven out of my mind
   By tenderness and desire!
Where are the torments? Where is love? Alas!
   For the unreturning days'
Sweet memory, and for the poor credulous
   Shade, I find no lament, no tears.

[1826]

CONFESSION

I love you – though it enrages me,
Though it is toil and pointless shame;
This hopeless stupidity
I pour out at your feet!
It doesn't become me and I'm too old! . . .
It's high time I was sensible!
Yet I recognize all the symptoms
Of the illness in my soul:
Without you I am bored – I yawn;
With you I am sad – I endure it:
The unendurable! What I'm saying,
My angel, is . . . I love you!
When I hear, coming from the drawing-room,
Your light step, or the rustle of
Your dress, or your innocent girlish voice,
Suddenly I'm like a simpleton.
You smile – it is joy;
You turn away – it is grief;
For a whole day of torment
Your pale hand is a recompense.
When, diligently yet nonchalantly,
You sit over your embroidery-frame,
Your eyes lowered, your locks swinging,
I gaze at you, content to be quiet,
Tenderly, like a child! . . .
Should I tell you of my unhappiness,
My jealous sorrow, when,
Sometimes even in bad weather,
You set out for a long walk – alone?
And the tears you shed in solitude,
And our talks in the corner,

And the journeys to Opochka,
And the piano in the evening? . . .
Alina! Have pity on me.
Perhaps, because of my sins,
I am not worthy of your love.
But pretend! Your glance can express
Everything so wonderfully!
Ah, it's not difficult to deceive me!
I want to be deceived!

[1826]

TO MY NANNY

COMPANION of my bleak days,
My dove, my frail darling nanny!
Alone in the deep pine-forest
You have waited and waited for me.
By the window of your upstairs room
You sigh like a sentry on watch,
And your knitting-needles move
More slowly in your gnarled hands.
You gaze at the forgotten gate,
At the black, distant road:
Yearning, forebodings, cares
Weigh down your breast, each hour.
Now you imagine . . .

[1826]

WINTER ROAD

Through the murk the moon is veering,
  Ghost-accompanist of night,
On the melancholy clearings
Pouring melancholy light.

Runs the troika with its dreary
Toneless jangling sleigh-bell on
Over dismal snow; I'm weary,
Hungry, frozen to the bone.

Coachman in a homely fashion's
Singing as we flash along:
Now a snatch of mournful passion,
Now a foulmouthed drinking-song.

Not a light shines, not a lonely
Dusky cabin . . . Snow and hush . . .
Streaming past the troika only
Mileposts, striped and motley, rush.

Dismal, dreary . . . But returning
Homewards! And tomorrow, through
Pleasant crackles of the burning
Pine-logs, I shall gaze at you:

Dream, and go on gazing, Nina,
One whole circle of the clock;
Midnight will not come between us,
When we gently turn the lock

On our callers . . . Drowsing maybe,
Coachman's faded, lost the tune;
Toneless, dreary, goes the sleigh-bell;
Nina, clouds blot out the moon.

[1826]

THE PROPHET

Parched with the spirit's thirst, I crossed
An endless desert sunk in gloom,
And a six-winged seraph came
Where the tracks met and I stood lost.
Fingers light as dream he laid
Upon my lids; I opened wide
My eagle eyes, and gazed around.
He laid his fingers on my ears
And they were filled with roaring sound:
I heard the music of the spheres,
The flight of angels through the skies,
The beasts that crept beneath the sea,
The heady uprush of the vine;
And, like a lover kissing me,
He rooted out this tongue of mine
Fluent in lies and vanity;
He tore my fainting lips apart
And, with his right hand steeped in blood,
He armed me with a serpent's dart;
With his bright sword he split my breast;
My heart leapt to him with a bound;
A glowing livid coal he pressed
Into the hollow of the wound.
There in the desert I lay dead,
And God called out to me and said:
'Rise, prophet, rise, and hear, and see,
And let my works be seen and heard
By all who turn aside from me,
And burn them with my fiery word.'

[1826]

S HE's gazing at you so tenderly,
Drowning you in sparkling conversation,
Gay and witty, and her eyes
Absorbing you with their yearning.
But last night she was using all her skill
To give me secretly her little foot
Under the tablecloth for me to caress.

[1826]

ARION

THERE were many of us on the ship;
Some were tightening the sail,
Others were plunging the powerful
Oars into the deep
Waters. Leaning calmly on the tiller,
Our skilful helmsman steered the loaded bark
In silence; and I – full of carefree faith –
I sang to the sailors . . . Billows
Were suddenly whipped up by a storm . . .
Both helmsman and sailor perished!
– Only I, the mysterious singer,
Cast ashore by the storm,
Still sing my former hymns, and dry
My wet clothes in the sun, beneath a rock.

[1827]

FRUITLESS and chance gift, my breath,
Why were you given to me,
And why were you condemned to death
By inscrutable destiny?

Who fashioned brain and eye and limb
From nothingness, and gave
My spirit an immortal dream
And knowledge of the grave?

I weep because the only sound
Is life's monotonous,
Sad, aimless, endless lull, the ground-
Swell of the universe.

[1828]

Young mare,
Pride of the Caucasian breed,
I love your wild spirit
But why are you rushing?
For you, too, the time has come;
Do not roll your skittish eye,
Do not fling your feet in the air,
Do not wilfully gallop
In the broad and level field.
Wait; I shall make you
Become docile beneath me:
I shall guide your run
Into a measured circle
With a shortened bridle.

[1828]

ANCHAR

The Poison-Tree

IN the greedy colourless desert,
On sun-red soil,
The anchar stands guard
Terribly – alone in the universe.

The nature of parched steppe
Gave birth to it on a day of wrath
And fed the dead green of its foliage
And its roots with poison.

Poison oozes through its bark,
At midday melting in the sun;
But hardens towards evening
To a thick transparent gum.

Even birds will not fly to it;
The tiger turns away: only
Black storm-winds brush past
The tree of death; and flee, infected.

If a rain-cloud in its wandering
Moistens its drowsy leaves,
The rain, already poisonous,
Drips into the burning sand.

But with a glance of authority
Man sent man to the anchar;
Obediently he set out on his way
And returned at dawn with the poison.

He brought back the deadly gum
And a branch of faded leaves;
And sweat from his pale brow
Poured from him in cold streams;

Brought his gift; then, fainting, lay
On the bast covering the tent-floor,
And the poor slave died at the feet
Of his invincible master.

But the king, in that poison steeping
His obedient arrows,
Sent with them destruction
To his enemies in distant lands.

[1828]

Do not sing to me again
Your songs of sad Georgia.
They bring to memory
Another life, a distant shore.

Your cruel songs bring close
The steppe, the night – the features
Of a distant, humble girl
In the moonlight.

I see you, and straightway
Her features disappear;
You sing . . . straightway
I imagine her.

Do not sing to me again
Your songs of sad Georgia.
They bring to memory
Another life, a distant shore.

[1828]

WINTER. What shall we do in the country? I greet
With questions my servant, bringing me my tea
In the morning: is it warm? Has the snowstorm died down?
Is there powder-snow on the ground, or not? And can I leave
My bed for the saddle, or would it be better
To browse through my neighbour's old journals till dinner?
There is powder-snow. And straightway to horse,
And we trot through the fields in the first light of day,
Our crops in our hands, hounds following behind us;
We watch the pale snow with attentive eyes;
We circle, scour the land, and at a late hour,
Having missed two hares, come home.
How delightful! Here's evening; the blizzard howls;
The candle burns dimly; the heart contracts and aches;
Drop by drop, I swallow the poison of boredom.
I try to read; my eyes slide over the letters,
While my thoughts are far away . . . I close the book;
I take my pen, and sit; by force I tear
From my slumbering muse incoherent words.
Sound does not match with sound . . . I lose all control
Over rhyme, over my strange handmaiden:
Limply my verse drags on, cold and misty.
Tired, I stop my struggle with my lyre
And go into the drawing-room; there I hear a conversation
About the coming elections, about the sugar factory;
The mistress of the house frowns just like the weather,
Nimbly plying her steel knitting-needles,
Or telling fortunes by the king of hearts.
Boredom! Thus, in seclusion, day follows day!
But if, towards evening, when I sit in a corner
Playing draughts, some unexpected family:
An old woman and two girls (two fair-haired, shapely sisters)
Drive from far away, in a carriage or covered sledge,
To our sad village, how our dark region livens up!
How life, my God, becomes full!

At first there are attentive side-glances,
Then a few words, then conversations too,
And afterwards friendly laughter, and songs in the evening,
And lively waltzes, and whispering at table,
And languid glances, and frivolous words,
Lingering meetings on the narrow staircase;
And the girl at twilight goes out on to the porch:
Her neck and bosom are uncovered, and the snowstorm
                              blows into her face!
But the snows of the north are not harmful to the Russian rose.
How hotly burns a kiss in frosty weather!
How fresh a Russian girl is in the powder of snow!

[1829]

WANDERING the noisy streets,
Entering the crowded church,
Sitting among wild young men,
I am lost in my thoughts.

I say to myself: the years will fly,
And however many are here, we shall all
Go down under the eternal vaults.
Someone's hour is already at hand.

Gazing at a solitary oak,
I think: this patriarch
Will outlive my forgotten age
As it outlived the age of my fathers.

When I caress a dear child,
I'm already thinking: goodbye!
I yield my place to you: it's time
For me to decay and you to blossom.

I say goodbye to each day,
Trying to guess
Which among them will be
The anniversary of my death.

And how and where shall I die?
Fighting, travelling, in the waves?
Or will the neighbouring valley
Receive my cold dust?

And though it's all the same
To the feelingless body,
I should like to rest
Closer to the places I love.

And at the grave's entrance
Let young life play,
And the beauty of indifferent nature
Never cease to shine.

[1829]

WINTER MORNING

Sunlight and frost: a matchless blend!
But you sleep on, my dearest friend –
It's time, my beauty, to awake:
If not for me, you northern star
Veiled in voluptuous languor, for
The dawn, for northern Aurora's sake!

Last night, gloom covered everything,
Remember; snow was blanketing
The moon, which only fleetingly
And mutely glimmered through the murk;
And sitting here, your mood was dark;
But now, this morning – come and see!

In the blue sky there's hardly one
Cloudlet; and gleaming in the sun,
A carpet stretched to the sky's edge,
The snow lies; all the tracks are lost,
But there's the forest, bathed in frost,
And the stream sparkles like a sledge.

Oh, if you wanted to, we could
Stay in today; it would be good
To muse beside the crackling fire.
The room with amber light is glowing.
But the green firs – just look! I'm going
To strap our sledge to the brown mare.

She's quivering with impatience, so
Quickly let's skim the morning snow
– Dear friend, dear sleepy girl – and see

The empty fields, and speed along
By woods grown dense since I was young,
And banks of rivers dear to me.

[1829]

I loved you; and perhaps I love you still,
The flame, perhaps, is not extinguished; yet
It burns so quietly within my soul,
No longer should you feel distressed by it.
Silently and hopelessly I loved you,
At times too jealous and at times too shy.
God grant you find another who will love you
As tenderly and truthfully as I.

[1829]

WHAT comfort for you in my name?
It will die like the sad plash
Of a wave breaking on some distant shore,
Like the sounds of night in a dense forest.

On the pages of your album
It will leave only a dead sign,
Like the vague traces of an epitaph
Carved in an unknown tongue.

What comfort for you? Long forgotten
Amidst the storms of new emotions,
It will not offer to your soul
Pure and tender memories.

But on a silent day of sorrow,
Speak my name in your grief. Just say:
There is a memory of me, there is
In the world a heart in which I live.

[1830]

FOR the shores of your distant home
You left this alien land;
I shall never forget it – a long time
I wept before you, my hands
Growing cold and numb
Tried to stop you leaving; I
Used every means I could
To prolong the anguish of goodbye.

But from our bitter embrace
You tore your lips away;
You called me to leave this place
Of dark exile for your own land.
You said: 'When we meet again
In the shade of olive trees
Beneath a sky that's always blue,
My dearest, we will share love's kiss.'

But there, alas, where the sky's
Vault shines with blue radiance,
Where the shadow of olives lies
On the waters, you have fallen asleep
Forever. Your beauty, your suffering,
Have vanished in the grave –
But the sweet kiss of our meeting . . .
I wait for it; you owe it me . . .

[1830]

INVOCATION

OH, if it is true that at night,
When the living rest,
And from the sky the moonlight
Glides over the graves, –
Oh, if it is true, that then
The quiet graves are empty,
I call your shade, I wait for you:
To me, my friend, come here . . . here!

Appear, beloved shade,
As you were before our parting,
Pale, cold, like a winter's day,
Disfigured by your last illness.
Come, like a distant star,
Like a faint sound, a breath of wind,
Or like a terrible vision,
I don't care: come here, come here!

I'm not calling you that I
May learn the secrets of the grave,
Nor because sometimes
I am tormented by doubts . . .
Only, longing,
I want to say, I still love you,
I am still yours: come here, come here!

[1830]

74

DEMONS

THE moon through total darkness hurrying
  Illuminates the snow in flight;
Clouds are whirling, clouds are scurrying,
Dark is the sky, and dark the night.
Across the open plain I'm driven;
The little bell goes *Ding-ding-ding* . . .
By holy dread my soul is riven,
Such emptiness is gathering.

'Coachman, drive them faster, faster!. . .'
'Can't, sir; they're too tired, you see;
I'm blinded by the blizzard, master;
The roads are drifting heavily;
Can't see the horses – lost the track, sir;
We're done for – we'll be frozen – whey!. . .
Some demon's got us – that's a fact, sir!
A demon's leading us astray.

'Look, there he is! He's teasing, blowing,
Spitting at me . . . Lord! this one's mean –
He's scared the horses – they'll be going
Headlong into some damned ravine;
He's right in front – Lord, isn't he frightening!
Dressed like a milestone (bloody queer);
There he goes, off again, like lightning!
God save us, master – that was near.'

The moon through total darkness hurrying
Illuminates the snow in flight;
Clouds are whirling, clouds are scurrying,
Dark is the sky, and dark the night.

We lurch in circles, strength declining;
Suddenly silent is the bell;
The team has halted . . . 'What's that shining?' . . .
'Tree-stump or wolf, sir – who can tell?'

The storm is howling, the storm is crying,
Drives itself harder, in despair;
The horses snort; away he's flying,
Only his eyes in the grey murk flare;
The horses strain upon their traces;
The little bell goes *Ding-ding-ding* . . .
I see, amidst the endless spaces,
A host of spirits, gathering.

Numberless and formless devils
In the blizzard's moonlit haze
Twirling in their murky revels,
As leaves swirl in November days . . .
So many! So many! And being carried
Whither? Why do they plaintively sing?
Is there a witch who's getting married?
Some goblin are they burying?

The moon through total darkness hurrying
Illuminates the snow in flight;
Clouds are whirling, clouds are scurrying,
Dark is the sky, and dark the night.
Swarm upon swarm of demons, streaking
On through this limbo without end,
And with their plaintive howls and shrieking
They pounce upon my heart, and rend.

[1830]

My rubicund critic, my full-bellied mocker,
Ever ready to rail at my desolate muse,
Come here, and sit beside me for a while,
Let's see if we can find a bit of pleasure . . .
Look before you: a few squalid hovels,
Beyond, the black earth, a sloping plain,
And over all a thick line of grey clouds.
Where are the bright cornfields, forests, brooks?
Near the low fence in our yard
Two puny saplings stand to charm the gaze.
Only two. And one of them was stripped bare
By the autumn rain, and the other's leaves, sodden
And yellow, will pile up in a puddle with the first gust.
That's all. Not even a dog prowls in the road.
Oh, here comes a peasant, with two women behind him:
Bareheaded, a child's coffin under his arm;
From afar he shouts out to the priest's lazy son
To call his father and open up the church.
'Hurry up! We haven't got all day!'

[1830]

A deaf man summoned a deaf man to be judged
By a deaf judge. The deaf man shouted:
'He stole my cow!' 'Rubbish!' the deaf man yelled.
'My late grandfather already owned that waste plot.'
    The judge ruled: 'To avoid shame,
Make the young man marry her, though the girl's to blame.'

[1830]

LINES WRITTEN AT NIGHT
DURING INSOMNIA

I can't sleep; no light burns;
All round, darkness, irksome sleep.
Only the monotonous
Ticking of the clock,
The old wives' chatter of fate,
Trembling of the sleeping night,
Mouse-like scurrying of life . . .
Why do you disturb me?
What do you mean, tedious whispers?
Is it the day I have wasted
Reproaching me or murmuring?
What do you want from me?
Are you calling me or prophesying?
I want to understand you,
I seek a meaning in you . . .

[1830]

FOUNTAIN AT TSARSKOYE SELO

THE girl has dropped the urn, and broken it on a rock.
Sadly the girl sits, and holds the empty shard.
But miraculously the water does not dry up;
The girl sits timelessly sad over the timeless stream.

[1830]

ECHO

SHOULD beast's or hunter's cry astound
Dumb woods, or thundercrack resound,
Or a girl's voice, beyond the mound,
Ring out in song – to everything
   At once an answering sound
   Through empty air you bring.

You hearken to the stormy fall
Of boulders, to the breakers' roll,
And to the rustic shepherd's call –
     And send reply;
For you, though, no response at all . . .
     And such am I.

[1831]

No, I don't miss the dissipated nights,
The moans and cries of a young bacchante
Writhing like a serpent in my arms
When, with fierce caresses and love-bites,
She hastens the moment of final spasm.

Dearer to me are you, my quiet friend,
How tormentingly happier I am with you,
When at long last you condescend
To yield to my pleas, tenderly, without rapture,
Cold, ashamed, scarcely responding to
My transports, avoiding them with your lips, your eyes,
More and more coming to life, until
At last you share my pleasure against your will.

[1832]

AUTUMN

A fragment

What does not enter then my drowsy mind?
Derzhavin

1

OCTOBER's come – the grove's already shaking
The last leaves from the naked branches; cold
Has breathed, the road's becoming frozen, still
The stream runs, babbling, beyond the mill
But on the pond the ice has taken hold;
My neighbour swiftly with his pack is making
For hunting-grounds where winter crops are flattened,
And sleeping woods are stirred by baying hounds.

2

This is my time: I don't like spring; its slush
And stench – the boring thaw. Spring sickens me;
My blood is in ferment, my mind and feelings
Are trapped by longings. I like stern winter better,
I love her snows: how smoothly, rapidly and freely
The sleigh glides when you're with a friend, and she
Is warm and fresh beneath her sable fur,
Pressing your hand . . . moonlit, she's trembling, flushed!

3

How thrilling to be gliding over the bland
Faces of rivers, steel-shod, those level mirrors!
And think of winter festivals' brilliant stir!
But there is a limit; Aprils, and Junes, of snow –

Why, even the bear holding out in his ice-cave
Is growing tired of it. You can't for a whole year
Sleigh-ride with young witches, or sit behind
The double windows, moping by the stove.

4

Summer, you beauty, I would be in love
With you, if it were not for heat, dust, flies,
Mosquitos. You torment us till we cannot think;
We are suffering from drought, like pastures;
There's nothing to us but the lust to drink
And refresh ourselves, and we miss winter, the old mother;
We who said goodbye to her with wine and pancakes
Now commemorate her with ice-cream and ice.

5

Ordinarily the days of late autumn are abused,
But I, dear reader, love her for her quiet beauty
That glows so modestly. I love her as one loves
A child unloved in its own family. To speak truth,
Of all the seasons of the year I welcome her alone.
There is much in her that is good, and I,
Who am not a vainglorious lover, have found
In my wayward fantasy something special in her.

6

How can I explain this? She pleases me
As sometimes, perhaps, you have been drawn to
A consumptive girl. Condemned to death, the waif
– Poor girl – declines, fades uncomplainingly,
Without resentment; a smile on her vanished lips.
She is inattentive to the waiting grave;
On her face a crimson colour's playing.
She is alive today – tomorrow, not.

7

Dejected season! enchantment to the eyes!
Your elegiac beauty and your mourning
Colours are dear to me: the sumptuous
Fading of the woods in purple and gold,
The wind and the fresh breeze in tree-tops, skies
Covered with rolling mists,
The tentative sun-ray, the first frost,
The grey winter's distant warnings.

8

And with every autumn I come into bloom
Afresh; the Russian cold is healthy for me;
I love again the daily air we breathe:
Sleep comes in its proper time, and so does hunger;
Lightly, joyously beats my heart, desires seethe,
Once more I'm full of life, happier, younger,
– Such is my organism (if I may be
Prosaic for a moment in a poem).

9

A horse is brought; the rider on its back
Clings fast to the flying mane,
And resonantly under its blistering hooves
The frozen valley echoes, the ice cracks.
But the short day fades, and fire burns again
In the forgotten grate, now flaring brightly,
Now smouldering. In front of it I read,
Or relish ideas, rolled around in my mind.

10

I forget the world; and in the sweet
Silence I'm calmed by my imagination
Sweetly, and poetry wakes in me; my soul,
Gripped by a lyrical excitement, trembles,

Resounds, as in a dream,
And seeks release at last in free expression –
And thronging towards me invisible are creation's
Familiar friends I did not think to meet.

11

Thoughts whirl audaciously in the mind,
Airy rhymes are running forth to meet them,
Fingers cry out for a pen, the pen for paper,
A moment – lines and verses freely flow.
So a ship slumbers in the stirless vapour,
But hark: sailors leap out, all hands are swarming
Up and down the masts, sails fill with wind;
The monster's moving and it cleaves the deep.

12

It sails. Where shall we sail? . . .

[1833]

IT's time, my friend, it's time! the heart is craving peace –
Days after days are flying,
And every hour bears off a fragment of our life, while we
Prepare to live . . . and suddenly, we die.
There is no happiness on earth, but there is peace
And freedom. Long have I, a weary slave,
Dreamt for myself a distant sanctuary
Of uncorrupted pleasures and of labour.

[1834]

I thought you had forgotten, heart,
Your ability to suffer pain.
That easy gift would come, I thought,
No more again! No more again!
Gone were the raptures and the griefs
And the dreams you half-believed . . .
But now I know, while beauty lives
So long will live my power to grieve.

[1835]

       . . . I have visited again
That corner of the earth where I spent two
Unnoticed, exiled years. Ten years have passed
Since then, and many things have changed for me,
And I have changed too, obedient to life's law –
But now that I am here again, the past
Has flown out eagerly to embrace me, claim me,
And it seems that only yesterday I wandered
Within these groves.

       Here is the cottage, sadly
Declined now, where I lived with my poor old nurse.
She is no more. No more behind the wall
Do I hear her heavy footsteps as she moved
Slowly, painstakingly about her tasks.

  Here are the wooded slopes where often I
Sat motionless, and looked down at the lake,
Recalling other shores and other waves . . .
It gleams between golden cornfields and green meadows,
A wide expanse; across its fathomless waters
A fisherman passes, dragging an ancient net.
Along the shelving banks, hamlets are scattered
– Behind them the mill, so crooked it can scarcely
Make its sails turn in the wind . . .

       On the bounds
Of my ancestral acres, at the spot
Where a road, scarred by many rainfalls, climbs
The hill, three pine-trees stand – one by itself,
The others close together. When I rode
On horseback past them in the moonlit night,
The friendly rustling murmur of their crowns
Would welcome me. Now, I have ridden out
Upon that road, and seen those trees again.

They have remained the same, make the same murmur—
But round their ageing roots, where all before
Was barren, naked, a thicket of young pines
Has sprouted; like green children round the shadows
Of the two neighbouring pines. But in the distance
Their solitary comrade stands, morose,
Like some old bachelor, and round its roots
All is barren as before.

                  I greet you, young
And unknown tribe of pine-trees! I'll not see
Your mighty upward thrust of years to come
When you will overtop these friends of mine
And shield their ancient summits from the gaze
Of passers-by. But may my grandson hear
Your welcome murmur when, returning home
From lively company, and filled with gay
And pleasant thoughts, he passes you in the night,
And thinks perhaps of me . . .

[1835]

EYES open wide, the poet weaves,
Blind as a bat, his urgent way;
But feels a tug upon his sleeve,
And hears a passing stranger say:
'Why do you betray the Muse
By wandering aimlessly, my friend?
Before you reach the heights, you choose
To gaze beneath you, and descend.
Blind to the great harmonious scheme
Of creation, you become possessed,
Too often, by some trivial theme,
And sterile fevers rack your breast.
A genius should look up – the duty
Of a true poet is to rise;
His dwelling-place should be the skies;
His theme and inspiration, beauty.'
– Why does a wind swirl through a dusty
Ravine and shake its stunted trees,
And yet a ship spread out its thirsty
Canvas in vain for a light breeze?
Why does an eagle leave the peak,
And, gliding past the church-spire, seek
The miserable tree-stump? Why
Did youthful Desdemona swoon
In the Moor's spasm, as the moon
In the night's shadow loves to lie?
Because for wind, and eagle's claws,
And a girl's heart, there are no laws.
The poet too, like Aquilon,
Lifts what he wants, and bears it on –
Flies like an eagle, heeds no voice
Directing him, spurns all control,
And clasps the idol of his choice,
Like Desdemona, to his soul.

[1835]

91

EXEGI MONUMENTUM

I have erected a monument to myself
Not built by hands; the track of it, though trodden
By the people, shall not become overgrown,
   And it stands higher than Alexander's column.

I shall not wholly die. In my sacred lyre
My soul shall outlive my dust and escape corruption –
And I shall be famed so long as underneath
   The moon a single poet remains alive.

I shall be noised abroad through all great Russia,
Her innumerable tongues shall speak my name:
The tongue of the Slavs' proud grandson, the Finn, and now
   The wild Tungus and Kalmyk, the steppes' friend.

In centuries to come I shall be loved by the people
For having awakened noble thoughts with my lyre,
For having glorified freedom in my harsh age
   And called for mercy towards the fallen.

Be attentive, Muse, to the commandments of God;
Fearing no insult, asking for no crown,
Receive with indifference both flattery and slander,
   And do not argue with a fool.

[1836]

II · Narrative Poems and Dramas

THE GAVRILIAD

THERE is a young Jewess whom I adore
Both for her earthly beauty and her soul.
Sixteen, dark brows, two supple girlish mounds
Rising and falling beneath her linen dress,
A leg for love, a jewelled row of teeth . . .
Jewess, why are you smiling? Why that blush
Spreading over your face? Darling, I'm sorry:
I don't mean you – it's Mary I'm describing.

Deep in the country round Jerusalem,
Far from frivolities of every kind,
A hidden beauty spent her days in peace.
Her husband was an honourable man,
An unskilled carpenter, old, and grey-haired.
Being the only workman in the village
He was kept occupied, in spite of his
Rather poor workmanship, both day and night;
So busy with spirit-level, saw, and axe,
He had no time to bother with the charms
Bestowed on him: neither the wanton ringlets
Falling in waves, as the vine curls her tendrils,
Nor those mysterious parts to him revealed
Morning and night – which, if he saw at all,
Reminded him, perhaps, of knotted wood.
Let's say he was a father to the girl;
A good provider; what's called 'a good husband'.

But from the heavenly heights the Omnipotent
Glanced in a friendly manner at Maria,
His handmaiden; took in her shapely bosom –
And, feeling a pleasant heat, in his deep wisdom

Resolved to bless the barren and forgotten
Vineyard with secret generosity.
And now the night has folded up the fields;
Mary is sleeping sweetly in her bed.
Spake the Almighty – and the virgin dreamed.
Heaven, to its furthest reaches, opened,
And myriads of immortal spirits blazed;
Innumerable seraphim fly round,
Cherubim are plucking at their harps;
Archangels, their heads bowed beneath their wings,
Are sitting in expectant silence. There
Before them rises, dark with excessive bright,
The throne of the eternal being. Now
The king Himself has flashed into their view . . .
All prostrate fall . . . The music of the harps
Is stilled. Mary, head bent, can scarcely breathe,
And trembles like a leaf, hearing God's voice:
'Daughter of Israel, most beautiful
Of all earth's daughters, – burning with desire,
I summon you to share my glory. You
Are chosen for a special destiny;
Prepare, my handmaiden; the bridegroom comes.'

  Again God's throne adorned itself in cloud;
Heaven rang with jubilee and loud hosannahs,
The harps began again with sweet preamble . . .
With her arms folded cross-wise on her breast
Submissively, and open lips, Maria
Stands facing heaven; her eyes gaze steadily
In one direction. Something is distracting,
Attracting, her – but what? Who, from the throng
Of courtiers, can't tear his eyes from her?
His superb raffish garb, the plumèd helmet,
His locks as golden as the shining wings,
His tall and languid stance, the bashful look –

Áll was to her taste. The warlike angel
Moved her, alone of all the multitude.
Gabriel, be proud! – The scene dissolved; like shadows
Born in a magic lantern, vanishing
Despite the children's pleas. Dominions, thrones,
Archangels, the cloud-clapped towers – all dissolved.

At dawn the lovely girl awoke, and nestled
Deeper into the languid warmth. Her dream,
And Gabriel, would not go from her mind.
She wanted to be pleasing to heaven's master,
Had not been unresponsive to his words,
Deeply respected him, – but Gabriel
Seemed more attractive . . . So, now and again,
A general's wife falls head over heels
In love with a strait-laced adjutant. It happens;
Everyone knows it does. What can one do?

Love is an enigma; let's talk about it
Awhile (it's the only talk I understand).
In days when someone's ardent gaze has stirred
Our blood up, when deceitful longings fire
Our hearts tormentingly and weigh our souls,
And we have one obsession, day and night –
Is this not true? – we hunt among our friends
For a confidant; and in his ear translate
The secret tongue of torturing love into
The sort of barrack-room talk he loves to hear.
Even when we have seized the wingèd moment
Of heavenly rapture and the modest girl
Is stretched back on the bed, when we have lost
The torment, and there's nothing to desire, –
We want to make it live again in memory,
We love to find our confidant, and chat.

And Thou, O Lord, didst know that turbulence,
And Thou didst burn like us, O God above.
The all-Creator cooled to his creation;
Prayers boring him, he composed psalms of love
And loudly sang: 'I love thee, Mary mine,
My immortality drags dully by . . .
Where are my wings? To Mary I shall fly
And on my beauty's breast I shall recline . . .'
And so on . . . Some, in oriental style,
To which He was addicted. Having called
His favourite, Gabriel, to his side, in prose
He talked about his love. Their conversation
Is indexed by the Church, or else St John
Left a hiatus in the manuscript.
But there's an Armenian legend which suggests
That God chose Gabriel as His go-between,
Hermes, or Mercury, dispatching him
At eventide to Mary. The archangel
Had enjoyed many a lucky mission, bearing
Orders and letters to and fro, which earned
Profit and honour; yet that had not quelled
His leaping ambition. The son of glory hid
His nature in a lavish show of being
A perfect servant – or, as we say, a pimp.

But Satan, the old enemy, is not sleeping!
Fluttering in the intense inane, he heard
That God was crazy for a Jewish girl,
Whose destiny would be to save our kind
From Hell's eternal torments. He was grieved
Bitterly by this news, and took steps. Meanwhile,
God sat in heaven, befuddled by a girl,
Forgetting the whole earth, which in the absence
Of His direction went its own sweet way.

What's Mary doing? Where's the unhappy wife
Of Joseph? – In her garden, pensive, sad,
She spends an innocent hour of leisure, and
Waits for the captivating dream's return.
A beauteous image will not leave her soul,
Her thoughts go flying up to Gabriel.
She daydreamed in the coolness of the palms,
Beside a rippling stream. The fragrant flowers
Do not delight her, nor the limpid waters . . .
Suddenly she sees – a gorgeous snake,
Entwined above her head in brilliant scales,
Gleaming and swaying amid shady branches.
He says to her: 'O Rose of Sharon, lily
Of the valley, stay! I'm your obedient slave . . .'
Is it possible? Wonder of wonders! Who
Is talking to the simple-hearted maid?
Alas, of course, the Fiend.

                        The serpent's beauty,
The exuberant flowers, his call to her, the fire
Of his deceitful eyes – all pleased Maria.
She spared him a soft glance, as if to slake
The drought of her young heart in idleness,
And fell into a dangerous conversation:

'Who are you, snake? Your smooth and flattering tongue,
Your radiant beauty and your flashing eyes,
Unless I am deceived, tell me you are
The one who lured our sister Eve to that
Mysterious tree, and plunged her into sin.
You ruined the poor, inexperienced girl,
And with her all of Adam's kin, and us.
We were forced down into an evil pit.
Aren't you ashamed?'
                   'Don't listen to the priests.

I did not ruin Eve, I rescued her.'
'You rescued her! From whom?'
       'From God.'
          'You villain!'
'He was in love with her, you see . . .'
        'Take care!'
'Burning with desire . . .'
      'Be silent!'
       'She
Was in grave danger . . .'
     'Snake, you lie!'
        'God's truth,
My dear. I swear –'
    'Don't take God's name in vain.'
'But hear me out . . .'

     Now Mary thought: 'It's wrong
To lurk here in the garden listening to
The slanders of a snake. My heavenly Father
Is guarding me, however, loving me,
And surely will not let His handmaiden
Be harmed, – for what? For talking! Nor will he
Allow me to be led into temptation.
And it's a modest-looking snake. So where's
The sin in it? Can it be evil? Stuff! –'
Thus did she think; and therefore lent an ear
For an hour, forgetting love and Gabriel.
The cunning demon, superciliously
Unwreathing his rattling tail, arching his neck,
Slid from the branches, and his beady eye
Looked up at her. He said:
      'I shan't attempt
To make my story fall in line with Moses':
He used a fiction to enslave the Jews;
A whopping lie is easier to believe

Than a small white one, and the Jews believed him.
And God rewarded him for toadying.
But I'm no court historian, believe me:
The important rank of Prophet doesn't tempt me!

'Like you, young Eve mooned about in the garden,
Delightful, modest, and intelligent,
Yet her bloom wasted in the desert air.
Just man and maiden, always face to face,
Upon the banks of Eden's shining rivers
Quietly and innocently living;
If you can call it life. Monotonous days
And tedious years. The shady grove, their youth,
Eternal leisure – should have provoked desire
In them, but did not. They walked hand in hand,
Drank, ate. The days were yawned away, and night
Brought them no lively joys, no passionate sport . . .
What can you say? The stern Judaic God,
Sullen and jealous, in love with Adam's wife,
Was keeping her for Himself. What a distinction!
What bliss! . . . To sit in heaven like a prison,
Or grovel at His feet with endless prayers,
Praising His goodness, wondering at His beauty,
Not daring even to glance at someone else,
Even in secret, flirting with an archangel . . .
This is the lot of the Creator's mistress.
And what's to come? The plainsong of old men,
Old wheezy sacristans, as a reward
For all the torturing boredom, the prayers of crones
Constantly irritating you, candles, and incense,
A jewelled ikon . . . O enviable fate!

'Well, I was so distressed at her position,
And liked the girl so much, I thought I'd better
Confuse their blank sleep, even at the risk

Of drawing the Creator's wrath upon me.
You've heard what happened? She dreamed vaguely of
Two apples hanging on a marvellous bough
(Love's happy and appealing symbol), and
The daydream stirred in her a vague desire;
She grew aware of her own loveliness,
Felt a luxurious tremble in the flesh,
With thudding heart she saw her friend was naked.
I watched them! I observed the wonderful
First steps of love, the science I had made . . .
Deep into the woods my couple wandered . . .
Where their eyes strayed their hands were quick to follow . .
Between the lovely legs of his young wife
Adam went seeking the discovered rapture,
And soon a raging fire was burning through him . . .
He wondered at the source of so much pleasure;
His soul caught fire too, and was lost in it;
Swept by the flames, her hair dishevelled, Eve,
With lips that barely moved from his sweet lips,
Clung to him with her legs, her arms, her spirit.
She swooned among the shady palms, the tears
Of love were on her cheeks – and the young earth
Covered with its blossom the first lovers.

'Until dawn broke they scarcely closed their eyes;
Then, until sunset, no endearing smiles
Wanted, nor youthful dalliance as beseemed
A husband newly crowned and his fresh bride.
You know the sequel. God shattered their delights,
Expelling them from paradise forever,
Hounding my couple from the land they loved,
Where they had lived untroubled for so long,
In innocence, embraced by lazy stillness.
But I had opened up the secret places
Of sensuality, youth's joyous rights,

Sweet carnal languor, raptures, tender words,
Kisses, and blissful tears. So tell me, now,
Did I betray her? And should Adam blame me?
Well, I don't know. I only know that Eve
Wanted to stay friends with me, and did.'

The Devil stopped. And Mary quietly
Considered Satan's slanders. Thought: 'Perhaps
He's right. I've heard it said you can't achieve
Happiness, bliss, with honours or with glory;
Nor can you buy it. Love is the only way . . .
Love! But how, and why, and what *is* love? . . .'
She'd listened with an aching concentration
To the whole story Satan had unravelled.
It glowed before her like a brilliant picture
With every image, every detail, clear
(For it was wonderfully new to her).
From hour to hour the vivid picture gained
Ever more colour in her imagination,
And suddenly the snake seemed to have gone –
Before her was another apparition:
She sees a beautiful young man, who kneels
At her feet, not saying a word, but flashing up
Eloquent eyes at her, asking for something.
One of his hands is offering her a flower,
The other fumbles at her simple dress,
Is up, in no time, underneath her clothes,
And a light finger playfully is feeling
In there for secret pleasures. It's all new,
All marvellous, to Mary, all confusing –
Complicated – but a shameless flush
Meanwhile has spread into her virgin cheeks,
A languid heat is running through her flesh,
Her young breast starts to pant, her heart to race;
She felt herself grow weak, and dumb. She shut

103

Her bewitching eyes, and let her head incline
On his breast, cried, 'Ah!' and sank down on the grass . . .

My dear friend! You to whom I dedicated
My early dreams of hope and my first yearning:
Beautiful girl, to whom I once was dear,
Will you forgive me these remembrances?
The sinful pastimes of my youthful days,
Those evenings in the bosom of your family,
When, near your strict, infuriating mother,
I troubled you with secret agitation
By enlightening your lovely innocence?
I taught your hand, so quiet, so submissive,
To cheat the heavy time of separation
And slake with sweet relief the hours of silence,
A maiden's agonizing sleepless night.
But now your youth with its rich bloom of beauty
Has dimmed, the smile has flown from your pale lips . . .
Will you forgive me, O my dearest friend?

Father of sin, Mary's insidious foe,
You are to blame for everything she did;
You loved the depravity, amused yourself
Arousing the Almighty's spouse, muddying
Her innocence through pure audacity.
Oh yes, you gloried in it! Plunge again,
Seize fast the livelong minute . . . Your time is close!
The light is fading, twilight's ray is done;
All's quietness. Over the weary girl
With shimmering murmuring wings the archangel stoops,
Love's emissary, heaven's brilliant son.

From horror at the sight of Gabriel,
The abashed beauty hid her face . . . The Prince
Of Darkness rose from her, discountenanced,

And said: 'Proud denizen of bliss, who sent
For you? Why have you quit the courts of heaven
And the ethereal heights? Why have you broken
The enchantment of a happy harmless couple?'
But jealous Gabriel, frowning, unamused
By this audacious and facetious greeting,
Said: 'You demented devil and apostate,
Ruined archangel, who preferred mournful gloom
To that celestial light, do you dare dazzle
Sweet Mary; then, cool as a cucumber,
Blame me? Be off with you at once, or I
Will make you skip!' 'Sycophants don't scare me . . .
Arselickers of the Almighty . . . Courtly pimps!'
Said the arch-fiend, malevolently glowing –
And suddenly struck the archangel in the teeth,
And Gabriel, with a cry, went reeling back;
He had to rest upon his left knee, dazed.
But found new strength from somewhere, rose, and hit
The adversary a surprise blow in the temple;
He cried out and went pale; then they were grappling,
First one, and then the other, gaining advantage,
But equally locked, a heaving entanglement,
Wheeling and staggering across the meadow;
Their chins into each other's chests they drove;
Sweating, grunting, crucifying each other,
With brute strength and with scientific cunning
Striving to throw the other and pin down.

You will recall that field I'm sure, my friends,
Where in our former days, having cut school,
In spring, we played at will, engaging in
Heroic combat. So did the angels now,
Until they were too spent to jeer or curse.
The infernal king cracked his broad shoulders, grunting,
But all in vain. Striving to end it all

105

With one blow, Satan knocked off the archangel's
Gold, plumèd helmet, glittering with diamonds.
He grips his silken locks, and bends him back
Agonizingly to the dry ground. Mary
Can only look on, also in agony,
To see her hero pinioned there. She trembles.
It looks all over. Hell prepares to cheer.
Quick-thinking Gabriel, though, is not done yet.
He bites his adversary in a place
Superfluous and vulnerable in battle,
The puffed-up member he has used to sin.
The devil fell, screamed out for mercy, and
Could scarcely limp back to the murk of hell.

The lovely girl had watched the awesome struggle
Almost without breathing. When the archangel turned,
Flush with his victory, streaked with sweat, towards her,
And gave her an affable and friendly smile,
She smiled back, and a flame played on her face.
His spirit overbrimmed with tenderness.
How good, how womanly, the Jewess was!

The messenger was blushing like a boy;
With holy words he gave voice to his feelings:
'O Mary immaculate, rejoice! Be glad!
Blessed among women, loveliest of wives!
A hundredfold your holy child is blessed.
He will save earth from death, and harrow hell . . .
But, from the depths of my heart, I do confess
His sire's a hundred times more blessed still!'
He kneeled before her yearningly and pressed
Her hand . . . She gazed at him with wistful eyes,
And sighed, and Gabriel drew her face to his
And kissed her. Silent, blushful, and confused,
She felt his hand glide smoothly to her breast . . .

'Please don't!' she whispered, but a wilder kiss
Stifled her last attempt to cry or moan . . .

How will their jealous God respond to this!
Gabriel, don't worry: Mary will handle it;
For women are the devotees of love,
Who can, with happy artistry, deceive
The bridegroom, take him in, distract him from
The merry hints and smiles of connoisseurs,
And scuffle all the tracks of pleasant sin.
Each mother well instructs her errant daughter
To simulate embarrassment and pain,
Shyness and ignorance, on that first night,
And each one plays the role superbly: then,
Come morning, she can feel a little better
About this dreadful thing she's never dreamed;
Still, she looks pale; her husband feels a brute
For having wreaked his selfish will on her.
Yet he feels cocky too, of course – so virile!
The mother whispers: 'Lord have mercy on us!' –
An old friend's tapping, smiling, at the window.

Already Gabriel's winging back to heaven
With the good news. God meets him anxiously,
Showering the exhausted servant with good will.
'How did it go?' 'Hard, I can tell you: hard.
I had to work on her; kept prodding, prodding . . .'
'But did it work? Did she say yes?' 'She did.'
At this the Lord of Heaven grew lost for words.
He rose from His throne and sent them all away
With a twitch of His brows, like Homer's god
Of old, whom all his numerous sons obeyed
Unquestioningly; but the Greek faith is dead,
Zeus dead; we live in more enlightened times.

In silence, thrilled by lively memory,
Mary lay resting on the rumpled sheet,
On fire still with voluptuousness and yearning.
Softly she calls on Gabriel, and prepares
The secret gift of love by kicking off
The coverlet. She looks down with a smile
At her own pleasant, excellent nakedness,
Marvelling at it. In tender reverie,
Languid and half-asleep, she falls to sin,
Drinking from the cup of consolation
With a serene enjoyment. Ah, Satan, Satan,
I can hear your laughter! But what's this now!
Suddenly a feathery white-winged dove
Flies in through the window and goes fluttering
Around her, striving to sing gay songs, and then
Darts down between her knees. He settles, quivering,
Above his rose; he pecks it, crawls around
And twirls about, his little feet and beak
Hard at it. So, He's come! – She realizes
She has to entertain another; pressing
Her knees together, the Jewess gave a cry,
Sighed, trembled, started to pray and weep,
But the dove has his way, billing and cooing,
Throbbing for joy of love, then falls away
In sleep, shading love's flower with a wing.

When he had flown off, Mary, exhausted, thought:
'What fun and games I've had! One, two, three! Who
Would not be tired? But I can say, I think,
I've stood the test. I've managed in one day
The devil, an archangel, and the Lord.'

Almighty God was well pleased with His son,
Begotten on the Jewish girl, but she
Continued to see Gabriel, lucky devil,

On the quiet. And Joseph was complacent,
Like many others, remaining a pure virgin,
Yet loving Christ as though he were his own,
For which the Lord rewarded him with joy.

Amen, amen! How can I end my story?
Putting off childish things, my roguery,
I pray you, wingèd Gabriel, keep me safe!
Long have I been a heretic in love,
Young goddesses insanely worshipping,
The demon's friend, a faithless hooligan.
Now bless my contrite heart. I'm not the same.
I have seen Helen: she is as lovely as
Sweet Mary; she's my queen for evermore.
Inspire my words to her, instruct me how
Best I may please, and light the spark of love
In her breast. Or else I will turn to Satan!
But days fly past, and time will scatter silver
On my head; my solemn wedding day will come,
Joining me at the altar with a loving
And much-loved wife. You gracious comforter
Of Joseph, I implore you on my knees,
When that time comes, grant me sound sleep, meekness,
Infinite patience towards my faithful wife,
Peace in my home and love for my fellow men.

[1821]

THE GYPSIES

THE Gypsies in a clamorous throng
  Wander round Bessarabia.
Tonight above a river-bank
They have spread their tattered tents.
Their camp-site is, like freedom, gay,
Peaceful their sleep beneath the heavens;
Between the wagon-wheels a fire
Is burning, and the family sits
Around it, cooking supper; horses
Graze in the bare field; behind
The tent a tame bear lies, unchained;
Everything's alive amid the steppes:
The peaceful labours of the family,
Ready to be off at dawn,
And women's songs, and children's shouts,
And the travelling anvil's clang.
But now, a sleepy silence falls
Over the nomad band; and one can hear
Only the bark of dogs, the neigh of horses,
In the brooding steppes. The lights
Everywhere are doused, all is quiet,
Only the moon is shining, high,
Shedding her twilight on the camp.
In one tent, an old man does not sleep;
He sits before the embers, warmed
By their last glow, and gazes out
At the distant fields, covered in night.
His daughter has gone rambling in
The desolate fields; she is inured
To coltish freedom, she will come back;
But it is night already, soon

The moon will leave that distant cloud –
Zemfira is still out; the supper
Her father's cooked for her is cold.

   But here she is. And after her
Across the steppe a young man hurries;
He is a stranger to the gypsy.
'Father,' the girl says, 'I bring a guest,
He was wandering on the steppe, I've asked him
To stay with us tonight. He wants
To be a gypsy like us; the law
Is hunting him; I'll be his friend.
His name is Aleko – he's
Ready to follow me everywhere.'

OLD MAN

I'm glad. Sleep here with us tonight
Under the shelter of our tent
Or stay with us longer if you wish.
Share with us our bread and roof.
Be one of us, learn to enjoy
Our wandering poverty and freedom;
Tomorrow morning at sunrise
We will move off in one wagon;
Find for yourself a task that suits you:
Forge iron and sing songs, and make
The rounds of the villages with the bear.

ALEKO

I'd like to stay.

ZEMFIRA

            He shall be mine –
Who will dare to drive him from me?
But it is light . . . the young moon
Has set; mist covers all the fields,
And I am overcome by sleep.

*

111

Daybreak. The old man quietly
Wanders around the silent tent.
'Get up, Zemfira: the sun is rising;
Wake up our guest; it's time, it's time! . . .
My children, leave the couch of bliss! . . .'
Noisily the tribe poured out,
The tents were taken down; the wagons
Were ready to start out once more.
The trek began; the wagon-wheels
Churned, rolled, into the empty plain.
Donkeys carry playful children
In panniers; husbands, brothers,
Wives, maidens – both old and young
Follow along; the noise of shouts,
Gypsy airs, the bear's roar,
His chain's impatient jangling;
The motley of garish rags,
Old men's and children's nakedness,
Dogs barking and yelping, the bagpipe's voice,
The wagons' creak; all wretched, wild,
Disorderly, and yet so briskly –
Restless, unlike our deathly pleasures,
This idle life as mournful as
The song of slaves under the lash!

Gloomily the young man gazed
At the deserted steppe, and dared
Not ask himself the reason for
His sorrow. Black-eyed Zemfira's there
Beside him, he's at liberty
And the sun beams cheerfully at noon;
Why, then, does the young man's heart
Quake? By what care is he oppressed? . . .

Tell me, my friend: you don't regret
What you have given up forever?

ALEKO

What have I given up?

ZEMFIRA
You know;
People you shared your life with, cities.

ALEKO

What is there to regret? If you
Could see those stifling cities!
There people stifle behind bars,
Don't breathe the cool morning, nor
The scent of the spring meadows;
They are ashamed of love and passion;
Bowing their heads before an idol
They trade their freedom, ask for chains.
What have I given up? The anguish
Of being betrayed, of being judged
By bigots, the mob's mindless howl,
The glitter of corruption.

ZEMFIRA
But
There are vast buildings, many-coloured
Carpets, games, rich feasts, and dresses –
The girls' dresses are so fine there –!

ALEKO

What of the pleasures of the city?
Where love is not, there are no pleasures.
As for the girls . . . you're lovelier,
Even without pearls and finery,
Without necklaces! My love, don't change

From what you are! My one desire
Is to share days and years of love
With you, and voluntary exile!

OLD MAN
Though you were born to luxury,
You like our life. But there are some
Who can't get used to freedom, after
A life of ease. We have a legend,
Handed down from age to age.
There was a man who had been banished
By his Emperor; he had to leave
His southern home and live among us
In exile. I used to know his name,
A queer sort of name, but I've forgotten.
He was already old, yet young
Still in his lively, innocent soul –
He had a marvellous gift for song
And a voice like the sound of rushing waters –
And everyone liked him. He lived
On the banks of the Danube, offending
No one, charming everyone with tales;
He did not understand anything,
And was weak and timid, like a child;
His neighbours, taking pity on him,
Caught game and fish for him; and when
The river froze and the wintry gusts
Blew, they found the saintly old man
Some furs to cover himself with;
But he could never accustom himself
To our poor life; he wandered around,
Pale and withered, looking lost.
He used to say an angry God
Was punishing him for his transgressions . . .
He waited for deliverance, grieved,

Walked along the Danube banks,
Wept every day, remembering
His far-off city. When he lay dying,
He asked that his dead body should
Be carried to the south: even
His bones, he thought, would hate to lie
In this foreign place.

ALEKO
Is this, then,
The fate of your sons, O Rome? Singer
Of love and of the gods, tell me
What is glory? A hollow sound
From the grave, a voice extolling life
From generation to generation
On-rushing? Or a wild gypsy's tale
Related in a smoky tent?

Two years go by. The gypsies wander
Still in their friendly noisy throng;
And, as before, they take their rest
And food, wherever pleases them.
Having thrown off the chains and shackles
Of enlightenment, Aleko lives
Freely like them; without regrets
Or cares he passed the roving days.
He is the same, the family too;
Not even recalling former years,
He has grown used to the gypsy habits.
He likes the shelter of the camp
At night, and the intoxication
Of everlasting unhurriedness,
And their frugal tuneful tongue. The bear,
A fugitive from home like him,

Ponderously dances, roaring,
And gnawing at the irksome chain,
Watched by a cautious crowd outside
A Moldavian homestead in the hamlet
Along the steppeland road; there, leaning
On his staff, the old man strikes
Unhurriedly the tambourine,
Aleko sings and leads the beast,
Zemfira flits around the village
Collecting the voluntary gifts.
Night falls; all three have cooked the millet
The day has gleaned; their shaggy guest,
The bear, is hanging round the tent.
The old man's gone to sleep – and all
Is peaceful in the tent, and dark.

The old man in spring sunlight warms
His cooling blood; his daughter sings
A love-song as she rocks the cradle.
Aleko listens and turns pale.

ZEMFIRA

Hoary man, hateful man,
Gash my frame, burn my frame:
Brave I am, scoff I can
At the knife, at the flame.

Thee as hell I abhor,
And despise heartily;
I another do adore,
And for love of him die.

ALEKO

What kind of stupid song is that?
Be quiet, I am sick of your singing.

ZEMFIRA

You needn't listen if you don't like it.
I'm singing it for myself, not you.

> *Gash my frame, burn my frame;*
> *Nothing I will tell thee;*
> *Hateful husband, my love's name*
> *Thou wilt not tear from me.*

> *He is fresher than the spring,*
> *Hot as summer days, he!*
> *How brazen is he, and how young!*
> *O how well he loves me!*

> *O how him I caressed*
> *In the night still and fine!*
> *O how then we did jest*
> *At that grey head of thine!*

ALEKO

Be quiet, Zemfira! I've had enough . . .

ZEMFIRA

So you have understood my song?

ALEKO

Zemfira!

ZEMFIRA

Be angry if you like,
I am singing the song about you.

[*Goes off singing* 'Hoary man', *etc.*]

OLD MAN

Yes, I remember, I remember.
That song has long been sung among
The gypsies roaming the Kagul steppes,
My Mariula used to sing it

117

Once in a while of a winter night,
Dandling her daughter before the fire.
In my mind the years gone by
Hour by hour grow darker, darker;
But that song stays with me, Aleko.

All is quiet; night. The moon
Has turned the southern sky to azure.
The old man is wakened by Zemfira:
'Oh, father! Aleko frightens me.
Listen: through his heavy sleep
He groans and sobs.'

OLD MAN
                        Do not touch him.
I have heard of an old Russian belief:
Now, at midnight, a sleeper's breathing
Is stifled by a domestic spirit;
Before dawn it will go away.
Sit with me quietly.

ZEMFIRA
                        He whispers:
'Zemfira!'

OLD MAN
                        He's searching for you, sleeping.
You are dearer to him than all the world.

ZEMFIRA
His love is stale to me. I'm bored;
My heart wants to be free – already
I . . . But hush! you hear? He's saying
Another name . . .

OLD MAN
                        Whose name?

ZEMFIRA

You hear?
Such a hoarse groan and violent gnashing . . .
How horrible! . . . I'll waken him . . .

OLD MAN

You shouldn't do; don't chase away
The night spirit – it will leave of itself . . .

ZEMFIRA

He has turned over, he's half-risen,
Calling me . . . He has woken up –
I'm going to him, – goodnight, go to sleep.

ALEKO

Where have you been?

ZEMFIRA

With father, talking.
Some spirit was plaguing you: your soul
Was suffering dreadfully in your sleep;
You frightened me: you ground your teeth
And called out to me.

ALEKO

I dreamt of you.
I dreamt that between us . . . I had
The most terrible dreams!

ZEMFIRA

Don't believe them.

ALEKO

Ah, I believe nothing: neither dreams,
Nor assurances, nor even your heart.

OLD MAN

Young madman, what are you sighing for?

Here we're all free, the sky is clear,
And the women are famed for their beauty.
Don't grieve; it doesn't suit you.

ALEKO

Father,
She does not love me.

OLD MAN

She is a child,
And you should treat her moods more lightly.
To you, love is a serious business,
But a girl's heart treats it as a joke.
Look up: look at the distant moon;
She sheds an equal radiance
On everything she passes over.
She will call briefly on a cloud,
Light it up brilliantly – but then
She's off again to another, where
She also won't stay long. And who
Shall appoint to her a place in heaven
And say: there you shall come to rest?
Who shall tell a young girl's heart:
Love one thing only, do not change?

ALEKO

How she loved me! How tenderly,
In the silent wilderness she leant
Towards me, and whiled away the night!
Yes, she is like a playful child –
How often she dispelled dark thoughts
In me with her bright chatter, or
Intoxicating kisses! . . . Now
She has grown cold to me; Zemfira's
Unfaithful . . .

OLD MAN

Listen: let me tell you
A story about myself. Long ago,
When the Danube was not yet enslaved
By the Moscal – (there, as you see,
There are things I can't forgive, Aleko).
We feared the Sultan in those days,
And a pasha ruled the Budzhak steppe
From the high towers of Ak-Kerman –
I was young; my soul was joyfully
Astir in those days; and amongst
My curls there was no strand of white;
Among the fair young maidens there
Was one . . . I took delight in her
As in the sun, for a long time,
And in the end called her my own . . .

Ah, like a falling star my youth
Flashed by! We fell in with a band
Of gypsies who were strangers to us,
They'd pitched their tents near ours, close to
A hillside, and spent two nights with us.
They went off on the third night, and,
Abandoning our little daughter,
Mariula went off after them.
I was fast asleep; when I was wakened
By the rising sun, my love was gone!
I search, and I shout out her name –
No trace of her. Zemfira cried
From hunger; I cried too; since then,
I have had no mind for any girl;
Never have I sought another lover,
And have not shared the lonely days
And nights with anyone.

ALEKO

Why didn't
You hurry after the ungrateful
Woman and plunge a dagger into
Her heart, and kill those who had wronged you?

OLD MAN

What good would it have done? Freer
Than a bird is youth; who has the power
To restrain love? To each in his turn
Joy is given, and then removed.

ALEKO

I'm not like that. I won't give up
My rights without a struggle! Or
At least I'll get some satisfaction
From taking my revenge. Oh no! –
Even if I found my enemy
Lying asleep above the depths
Of the ocean, I would not spare the villain.
I'd thrust him into the sea, and laugh
At the sudden horror of his waking,
And I would enjoy the sound of his fall,
Exult in it, with a clear conscience.

YOUNG GYPSY

One more . . . one more kiss . . .

ZEMFIRA

It's time:
My husband's in a spiteful mood.

GYPSY

Just one . . . but longer! To say goodbye.

ZEMFIRA

Goodbye, before he comes.

GYPSY
                        But when
Will you come to me again?

ZEMFIRA
                        Tonight,
When the moon rises. There,
Beyond the mound above the grave . . .

GYPSY
You'll break your promise; you won't come!

ZEMFIRA
I'll come, my love . . . Now run! He's here!

   Aleko is asleep. Confused
Are the visions flickering in his mind;
He wakes in the darkness with a cry
And stretches his hand out, but it grasps
The cold blanket: *she* is not there . . .
Shuddering, he half-rises, listens;
Everything is quiet; waves
Of heat and cold run through his flesh;
He gets up, leaves the tent, and paces
Dementedly about the wagons. The moon
Is hidden in the murk, and all
Is dark and peaceful; a scattering
Of stars sheds a dim light; it brightens;
And in the dew Aleko sees
A faintly discernible trail that leads
Towards the far-off mounds; he strides
Impatiently towards them, though
His heart is filled with dread.

                        A tomb
Shines whitely in the distance, and

It draws his faltering steps . . . His lips
Tremble, his knees feel shaky, he
Is haunted by presentiment,
But walks on . . . Suddenly – or does
He dream it? – he can see two figures
Over the desecrated grave,
And hears them whispering.

FIRST VOICE

It's time . . .

SECOND VOICE

Stay . . .

FIRST VOICE

I can't. It's time, my dear.

SECOND VOICE

Stay until dawn.

FIRST VOICE

It's late already.

SECOND VOICE

You're a coward. One minute more.

FIRST VOICE

No, it would ruin everything.

SECOND VOICE

A minute!

FIRST VOICE

What if my husband wakes
While I am gone? . . .

ALEKO

He is awake.

Don't go, you two. There is no need.
This is a fine place, here by the grave.

ZEMFIRA

My love, run, run . . .

ALEKO

Where are you going,
My young peacock? Lie there!

[*Thrusts a knife into him.*]

ZEMFIRA

Aleko!

GYPSY

I am dying . . .

ZEMFIRA

You have killed him, Aleko!
You're covered in blood! What have you done?

ALEKO

Never mind. Now breathe his love.

ZEMFIRA

Enough; I'm not afraid of you!
I despise your threats, I curse your murder . . .

ALEKO

Die then, you too!

[*Stabs her.*]

ZEMFIRA

I die in love . . .

The morning star shone in the east.
Near the mound, a knife in hand,

Covered in blood, Aleko sat
On the gravestone. Two corpses lay
Before him. An abashed throng of gypsies
Surrounded him. Some distance off
They were digging a grave. The women came
In a sorrowing procession past
The dead lovers and kissed their closed eyes.
The old father sat alone and gazed
At his daughter without seeing her.
The bodies were lifted up, carried,
And put to rest in earth's chill lap.
Aleko watched it all, from a distance.
But when the bodies had been covered
With the last handful of earth, silently
And slowly he leaned forward and
Fell from the stone on to the grass.

Then the old man approached and said:
'Leave us, arrogant man! Leave us.
We are savages; we have no laws.
We do not torture, nor put to death –
We have no need of blood and groans.
But we will not live with a murderer . . .
You were not born for the life of the wild,
You crave freedom for yourself
Alone. Dreadful will be your voice
To us: we are timid and goodnatured,
You are strong and fierce – leave us then;
Farewell, and peace be with you.'

He spoke – and in a noisy throng
The nomads struck camp and departed
From the vale of that dreadful night.
Soon all had vanished in the wide
Vistas of the steppe. A single wagon,

Covered with a poor rug, stood
In the fateful field. Thus, sometimes,
Before winter, at the foggy time
Of morning when there rises from
The fields a flock of tardy cranes,
Which soars off southwards, crying,
One, pierced by the fatal lead,
Will stay behind, its hurt wing hanging.
Night came on; in the dark wagon
No one laid a fire, no one
Rested in sleep until the dawn.

Epilogue

By the magic power of song,
Hazy memories have revived
Of sunny, and of mournful, days.
In the land where long the dreadful
Clamour of arms was never stilled,
Where our old two-headed eagle
Still rustles with its bygone glory,
Staking new frontiers to the south,
I used to meet amid the steppes
On the boundaries of ancient forts
The peaceful wagons of the gypsies,
The children of a humble freedom.
In the waste lands I often roamed
Behind their idly moving swarms,
Shared their simple food at night
And fell asleep before their fires.
On those slow treks I learned to love
The joyous rhythms of their songs –
And for a long time Mariula's
Tender name rang in my thoughts.

But, even among you, there is
No happiness, poor sons of nature! . . .
Even beneath your tattered tents
There are tormenting dreams and visions,
Your nomad shelters in the wilds
Have not escaped misfortunes, and
Everywhere fateful passions swarm
And no one can resist the fates.

[1824]

THE BRIDEGROOM

FOR three days Natasha,
The merchant's daughter,
Was missing. The third night,
She ran in, distraught.
Her father and mother
Plied her with questions.
She did not hear them,
She could hardly breathe.

Stricken with foreboding
They pleaded, got angry,
But still she was silent;
At last they gave up.
Natasha's cheeks regained
Their rosy colour,
And cheerfully again
She sat with her sisters.

Once at the shingle-gate
She sat with her friends
– And a swift troika
Flashed by before them;
A handsome young man
Stood driving the horses;
Snow and mud went flying,
Splashing the girls.

He gazed as he flew past,
And Natasha gazed.
He flew on. Natasha froze.
Headlong she ran home.
'It was he! It was he!'

She cried. 'I know it!'
I recognized him! Papa,
Mama, save me from him!'

Full of grief and fear,
They shake their heads, sighing.
Her father says: 'My child,
Tell me everything.
If someone has harmed you,
Tell us . . . even a hint.'
She weeps again and
Her lips remain sealed.

The next morning, the old
Matchmaking woman
Unexpectedly calls and
Sings the girl's praises;
Says to the father: 'You
Have the goods and I
A buyer for them:
A handsome young man.

'He bows low to no one,
He lives like a lord
With no debts nor worries;
He's rich and he's generous,
Says he will give his bride,
On their wedding-day,
A fox-fur coat, a pearl,
Gold rings, brocaded dresses.

'Yesterday, out driving,
He saw your Natasha;
Shall we shake hands
And get her to church?'

The woman starts to eat
A pie, and talks in riddles,
While the poor girl
Does not know where to look.

'Agreed,' says her father;
'Go in happiness
To the altar, Natasha;
It's dull for you here;
A swallow should not spend
All its time singing,
It's time for you to build
A nest for your children.'

Natasha leaned against
The wall and tried
To speak – but found herself
Sobbing; she was shuddering
And laughing. The matchmaker
Poured out a cup of water,
Gave her some to drink,
Splashed some in her face.

Her parents are distressed.
Then Natasha recovered,
And calmly she said:
'Your will be done. Call
My bridegroom to the feast,
Bake loaves for the whole world,
Brew sweet mead and call
The law to the feast.'

'Of course, Natasha, angel!
You know we'd give our lives
To make you happy!'

They bake and they brew;
The worthy guests come,
The bride is led to the feast,
Her maids sing and weep;
Then horses and a sledge

With the groom – and all sit.
The glasses ring and clatter,
The toasting-cup is passed
From hand to hand in tumult,
The guests are drunk.

BRIDEGROOM
'Friends, why is my fair bride
Sad, why is she not
Feasting and serving?'

The bride answers the groom:
'I will tell you why
As best I can. My soul
Knows no rest, day and night
I weep; an evil dream
Oppresses me.' Her father
Says: 'My dear child, tell us
What your dream is.'

'I dreamed,' she says, 'that I
Went into a forest,
It was late and dark;
The moon was faintly
Shining behind a cloud;
I strayed from the path;
Nothing stirred except
The tops of the pine-trees.

'And suddenly, as if
I was awake, I saw
A hut. I approach the hut
And knock at the door
– Silence. A prayer on my lips
I open the door and enter.
A candle burns. All
Is silver and gold.'

BRIDEGROOM
'What is bad about that?
It promises wealth.'

BRIDE
'Wait, sir, I've not finished.
Silently I gazed
On the silver and gold,
The cloths, the rugs, the silks
From Novgorod, and I
Was lost in wonder.

'Then I heard a shout
And a clatter of hoofs . . .
Someone has driven up
To the porch. Quickly
I slammed the door and hid
Behind the stove. Now
I hear many voices . . .
Twelve young men come in,

'And with them is a girl,
Pure and beautiful.
They've taken no notice
Of the ikons, they sit
To the table without
Praying or taking off

133

Their hats. At the head,
The eldest brother,

At his right, the youngest;
At his left, the girl.
Shouts, laughs, drunken clamour . . .'

BRIDEGROOM
'That betokens merriment.'

BRIDE
'Wait, sir, I've not finished.
The drunken din goes on
And grows louder still.
Only the girl is sad.

'She sits silent, neither
Eating nor drinking;
But sheds tears in plenty;
The eldest brother
Takes his knife and, whistling,
Sharpens it; seizing her by
The hair he kills her
And cuts off her right hand.'

'Why,' says the groom, 'this
Is nonsense! Believe me,
My love, your dream is not evil.'
She looks him in the eyes.
'And from whose hand
Does this ring come?'
The bride said. The whole throng
Rose in the silence.

With a clatter the ring
Falls, and rolls along
The floor. The groom blanches,
Trembles. Confusion . . .
'Seize him!' the law commands.
He's bound, judged, put to death.
Natasha is famous!
Our song at an end.

[1825]

COUNT NULIN

It's time, it's time! the horns ring clear;
Already sitting on their steeds
Are whippers-in, in hunting gear;
The borzois tangle in their leads.
The squire stalks out on to the porch,
Flailing his arms, surveys his team.
First light. His face is like a torch,
Shining with pleasant self-esteem.
In Cossack coat he cuts a dash,
A Turkish knife's stuck in his sash,
In his bosom's a little flask
Of rum; a horn swings on a small
Bronze chain. In nightcap and a shawl
His wife stands at the pane to stare
Crossly at the bustle; they're
Nothing but children off to play;
Her husband has mounted eagerly,
Shouts to her: Don't wait up for me!
Digs in his spurs and rides away.

September moving towards its close
– To speak in tones of sober prose –
It's dreary in the country: mud,
Foul weather, autumn wind, fine snow,
Wolves howl. – But all this stirs the blood
Of huntsmen! They would rather go
From luxury to farthest fields,
Find their night's billet anywhere,
Grumble, get soaked, joy at the peals
That signal death to fox or hare.

But what can the spouse without a spouse
Do all day in the lonely house?
There's little she can find to do:
Storeroom and cellar to look into,
Mushrooms to pickle, geese to feed,
Dinner and supper to prepare, –
The housewife's eye is like a needle
Quick to find duties everywhere.

Unfortunately our heroine
(Oh, I forgot to give her name!
Natasha her husband called her, I'm
Not sure that I may do the same:
Rather, Natalia Pavlovna)
Natalia Pavlovna, alas,
Brought up by Madame Falbalat,
The emigrée, in her upper-class
Girls' boarding-school, without a training
In patriarchal discipline,
Wasn't much good at these, disdaining
Such dreary tasks within the home.

She's sitting in the window nook
With a sentimental book
Resting open in her hand:
Love of Elisa and Armand,
A novel in letters, volume four –
A classical, old-fashioned story,
Immensely long, admonitory
In a good-mannered, pious way,
Not too disturbing or obscure.

Natalia Pavlovna at first
Was reading it with interest,

But soon somehow was drawn away
To where farm-dog and billy goat,
Straight before the window, fought,
And quietly she watched the fray.
Round the fracas some boys were chuckling;
Meanwhile, under her sill, a flock
Of turkey-hens were sadly clucking,
Following after a wet cock.
Three ducks puddled; an old nurse
Walked across the miry ground
To hang up washing; snow around;
By moments the weather growing worse . . .
Suddenly a sleigh-bell's sound.

He who has lived too long apart
In such a place, friends, knows too well
How agitated grows the heart
At times, hearing a distant bell.
Is it the friend who keeps at last
A promise made in the bright past?
Is it – O God! – announcing *her*?
Closer and closer . . . the heart beats . . .
But, floating by, the sound retreats
Behind the hill, and is no more.

So was it with Natalia – she
Runs flustered to the balcony,
Looks and sees – beyond the river,
Close to the mill, a carriage creeps,
It's on the bridge – towards us! No;
It has turned left; she sees it go
Slowly away; and almost weeps.

But suddenly – oh joy! – disaster;
A slope; it's toppled. 'Filka! Vaska!

Come quick! That overturned *kolyaska* –
Bring it straight here, invite the master
To dinner. Run! Faster! Faster!
He may be dying! . . .'
                            The servant scurries
Away. Natalia Pavlovna hurries
To don a shawl and fix her hair,
Draw the curtain, move a chair.
'Oh Lord, I'm shaking. Give me strength.'
Here they come driving up at length.
Mournful, spattered with mud and snow,
Dragging itself along somehow,
A gravely wounded equipage.
Behind it a young gentleman
Is limping. His indomitable man
Is murmuring: *allons, courage!*
They're at the porch; they're in the hall.
Well, it's most kind . . . they're ready for
Emergencies; the linen's all
Been aired; they open wide the door.
While Picard's bustling with French zest,
The Count calling to be dressed,
Shall I describe for you this lord?
Count Nulin, new back from abroad,
Where like storms in March he chose
To blow his future revenues;
Like a fabled beast he is
For show, soon, in Petropolis
With a supply of morning suits,
Cloaks, corsets, fancy waistcoats, hats,
Fans, pins, cufflinks and lorgnettes,
Handkerchiefs bedecked with flowers,
Deluxe socks, awful tomes from France,
Albums of vile caricatures,
Sir Walter Scott's brand-new romance,

Jokes that everywhere are ringing,
Songs that everyone is singing,
That choice Rossini aria,
Et cetera, et cetera.

    The table's laid with appetizing
Dishes getting cold. It's late.
How much longer must she wait?
The door lets in the Count to dine.
Natalia Pavlovna, half-rising,
Politely asks, is he all right?
How about his leg? It's fine.
He goes to table, takes a chair,
Directs his instrument at her
And starts a conversation. He
Scolds Holy Russia. Heaven knows
How one can bear life in her snows.
To be in Paris now! Damnation!
'Ah yes, the stage.' '– That's lamentable!
C'est bien mauvais, ça fait pitié.
Talma has grown deaf and feeble,
And Mamselle Mars is scarcely able
To speak her lines. There's Potier
Of course, thank God; without a doubt
Potier now dominates the scene.'
'What authors are being talked about?'
–It's all Prévot and Lamartine. –
'Here too they're being imitated.'
– No! Really? Is the Russian mind
Beginning to grow sophisticated?
Here, in the country of the blind! –
'How are the waistlines?' – Extremely low,
Almost to . . . here, I'd say, just now.
Allow me to inspect your . . . yes . . .
Flounces, and ribbons . . . tracery . . .

That's quite a fashionable dress. –
'We get the *Telegraph*.' – I see!
Have you heard this charming chorus? –
And the Count sings. 'There's trifle still,
Count, *do* . . .' – No, no, I've had my fill. –

They rise from table. The young hostess
Is in the mood for pleasantries;
The Count, forgetting about Paris,
Is astonished at how nice she is!
They don't know where the time has fled;
The Count is ill at ease. Her eyes
Are now inviting him to bed,
Now are unresponsive – dead,
In fact. It's midnight, to your surprise,
Outside. The footman's snoring in
The hall, the neighbour's cock begins,
The watchman beats the iron plate;
The candles, weakening, start to flare.
Natalia rises from her chair:
'It's late, good night: our beds await.
Sleep well . . .' Rising with chagrin,
The half-enamoured Count Nulin
Kisses her hand. Is this, then, all?
Is the flirtation at an end?
– God forgive the flighty girl!
Softly she presses the Count's hand.

Natalia Pavlovna is undressed;
Before her stands Parasha. She,
My friends, preserves within her breast
More than Natalia's diary;
Washes, sews, and carries notes,
Asks for her lady's worn housecoats,
Romps with her master, shares a laugh,

Then screams at him – just like a wife –
And tells her mistress lies, of course.
She offers now a grave discourse
Relating all she knows about
The Count's affairs. The things she's learned!
She doesn't leave a stone unturned.
Natalia Pavlovna said 'Stop!'
At last. 'I'm sick of it. Enough!'
Asked for her nightgown and nightcap,
Lay down, and sent Parasha off.

Meantime, while this is going on,
The Count's undressed too by his man.
He lies down; fancies a cigar
And summons one; Monsieur Picard
Brings a silver glass, decanter,
Cigar, alarm clock, bronze
Candlestick, some tweezers, and a
Novel, an uncut romance.

Lying in bed, Sir Walter Scott
He's skimming with his eyes. The Count's
Distracted by a troubling thought:
'Can this be really love, for once?
May it be possible? . . . What a caper!
Still, it would be rather nice.
She's fond of me, that's obvious.' –
And therewith Nulin snuffed the taper.

Intolerable fever. He
Tosses and turns – the devil, waking,
Teases with wicked fantasy
Our fiery hero till he's shaking
From what, in his imagination,

He sees: her speaking invitation
Of gaze, her figure, rather full,
Her womanly and pleasing voice,
Good health's reflection in her face,
The russet of the country girl.
Recalls the tip of her dainty foot,
And the stage-managed carelessness
With which she pressed his hand – like this!
Just so! Nulin, you idiot,
Why did you leave? You had it made!
But it was not too late. Her door
Now, naturally, would be ajar . . .
And forthwith climbing out, and fumbling
For his silk robe of many hues,
He sets out in the darkness, stumbling
Over a chair, no time to lose
If he's to lie in the white fleece
– A new Tarquin to Lucrece.

So, sometimes, a sly avid cat,
The dainty darling of the house,
Steals from the stove to catch a mouse:
Stealthily walks, his ears laid flat,
Stalks it with his half-closed eyes,
Gathering himself, with twitching tail,
Cunningly unsheathes his claws
– Scritch-scratch, crunch, he doesn't fail.

The flushed Count finds his way by touch,
Groping through the dark; desire
Excites and tortures him so much
He can't breathe; trembles as the floor
Creaks under him . . . he waits . . . once more
Creeps on; and finds the private door.
Feels lock, brass handle, now his hand

Presses the handle softly, and
It yields as though by invitation;
He looks: a lamp is barely lending
The bedroom faint illumination;
The lady without perturbation
Is fast asleep, or is pretending.

He enters, thinks of a retreat,
Hangs fire – has fallen at her feet.
She . . . But now, with your permission,
Ladies of Petersburg, I ask you:
Imagine Natalia Pavlovna
Waking in this night of horror:
Decide for her what she should do.

She, opening her eyes wide, stares
Vaguely at him – our hero pours
Exquisite feelings in her ear,
And with emboldened hand's about
To touch the blanket, taking her
So by surprise she cannot stir
A limb . . . suddenly comes out
Of her dull trance, and full of proud
Anger, and terror too, perhaps,
Springing away in bed, she slaps
Tarquin – yes, slaps him! Slaps him hard!

Count Nulin's temper was aflame
To have swallowed such a shame.
I don't know what he might have done,
But a dog began to bark,
The shaggy Pomeranian,
So loudly even Parasha woke.
Hearing a servant's footsteps rustling,
Cursing his billet of the night,

And the bewitching little hussy,
The Count turned to ignoble flight.

How he, the mistress, and Parasha,
Spent the time till it was light,
You may imagine in your fashion;
I don't intend to set you right.

The Count is thoughtful in the morning,
Lazily himself adorning,
Gives his nails a manicure
In a half-hearted manner, yawning,
Ties his tie with negligence,
Doesn't smooth his lovely hair
With a hairbrush sprayed with scents.
I don't know what he thinks about.
But here they've called him down to tea.
It might be best to walk straight out;
Awkward, embarrassed, angry, he
Goes down to tea.
                    The young scapegrace,
Smiling, not looking in his face,
Biting her crimson little lips,
Talks about this and that, shines once
Her gaze full on him as she sips;
Confused by this turn of events
At first, he gradually cheers up,
Smiles back. She pours another cup.
He's joking with her affably.
In half an hour he's half in love
Again. – A noise. Who can it be?
'Natasha, hi!'
                    – Oh heavens above . . .
Count, this is my husband. Dear,
Count Nulin. –

'I'm delighted . . .
What dreadful weather! what a night! I'd
Half expected you were here –
Your coach is at the blacksmith's shop
Quite ready . . . Natasha! we tracked down
A hare near the orchard! Count, do stop
And have some of our vodka. Hey!
Vodka!' – I should be on my way. –
'Oh please. You won't find this in town;
We had it sent; it's good, you'll see!'
– No, truly, I have an appointment. –
'My wife and I like company.
Do stay!'
        But out of disappointment,
The loss of all his hopes, resentment,
The melancholy Count won't budge.
Already strengthened with a glass,
Picard's struggling with a case,
Two of Count Nulin's footmen trudge
Already to the coach, screw down
The trunk. Picard stows everything.
Coach at the porch, the Count has gone.
And with his going the story ends;
Except for a few words, my friends.

  Almost before the carriage rolled
Away into the snow, she told
Her husband all, and told a host
Of acquaintances and neighbours after.
But who loved Nulin's exploit most,
And most responded to her laughter?
You'll never guess. 'The husband, surely?'
No, not the husband. He was surly,
Took great offence – the Count's a fool,
A milksop! he would make him squeal

If he dared show his face again;
He'd set the hounds on him. Lidín
It was who laughed, the twenty-four-
Year-old landowner from next door.

Now with justice we may claim,
Friends, that in Russia may be found
Wives who cherish their good name
And do not fling their favours round.

[1825]

MOZART AND SALIERI

SCENE I

A Room.

SALIERI:

MEN say there is no justice on earth;
I say there's none in heaven either.
That's as clear to me as a simple scale.
I came into this world loving art;
While yet a child I listened, and I
Never wearied of listening, to
The organ ringing out, high up in
Our ancient church – my tears flowed sweetly
And of their own accord; I banished,
Early in life, frivolous pastimes;
Studies that were not music I scorned
Obstinately and haughtily, I
Dedicated myself to music
Alone. The first step was difficult,
The first path dull. But I overcame
Early reverses and established
Craftsmanship as a pedestal
For art; I became a craftsman; I
Lent an obedient and arid
Agility to my fingers and sureness
To my ear. Killing the sounds,
I dissected music like a corpse.
I checked harmony by algebra.
Then, certain of my technique, at last
I indulged the joys of creative
Fantasy. I began to create,
But on the quiet, in secret, not
Yet daring to dream of glory. How

Often, having sat in my silent
Cell for two or three days, forgetting
Both sleep and food, having tasted
The rapture and tears of inspiration,
I would burn my work and coldly watch
My thoughts, and the sounds I had given
Birth to, blaze and disappear in
A wisp of smoke! What am I saying? When
The great Gluck appeared and revealed
To us new secrets (deep, enchanting
Secrets), did I not cast aside all
That I had so ardently believed,
And did I not follow firmly and
Boldly after him, uncomplaining,
Like one who has got lost and is sent
In a different direction by
Someone he meets? By vigorous and
Intense persistence I at last reached
A high peak in the limitless range
Of art. Fortune smiled; I found within
Men's hearts the same harmony as in
My own creations. I was happy:
In peace I enjoyed my toil, success,
And fame, as well as the toil and
Successes of my friends and comrades
In this wondrous art. Never did I
Know envy – oh, never – neither when
Piccini captivated the ears
Of the philistine Parisians,
Nor when I heard for the first time
The opening chords of *Iphigenia*.
Who will say that proud Salieri
Was a contemptible envier,
A serpent trampled on by men, yet,
Still alive, impotently gnawing

Sand and dust? But now – I will say it
To myself – I am envious. I
Envy. O heaven! where is justice,
When the sacred gift, when immortal
Genius, is sent not to reward
Self-sacrifice, burning love, toil,
Ardour, supplications, but illumines
The head of a madcap, an idle rake?
O Mozart, Mozart!

MOZART: Oh, you saw me coming!
Shame! I was going to treat you to a joke.

SALIERI:
You! Have you been here long?

MOZART: No, I've just come.
I was on my way to see you and was bringing
One or two things to show you; but passing an inn
I suddenly heard a violin . . . Salieri,
My friend! you've never in all your life heard
Anything funnier! A blind fiddler in the inn
Was playing *Voi che sapete*. I was amazed!
I couldn't let you not hear it; I've brought him along
To give you a treat. Come in!

      [*Enter a blind man with his violin*]

                                Play us a trifle
From Mozart!

[*The old man plays an aria from Don Giovanni;* MOZART
                roars with laughter.]

SALIERI: And you can laugh!

MOZART: Ah, Salieri!
  I hoped you'd laugh too.

SALIERI: No, I do not
  Find it funny when some second-rate
  Painter daubs a Raphael Madonna
  For me; I do not find it funny
  When a contemptible fool slanders
  Alighieri with a parody.
  Be off, old man!

MOZART: Wait: take this, drink my health.

            [*Exit old man.*]

  You're in a bad mood, Salieri, I can see.
  I'll come another time.

SALIERI: What have you brought me?

MOZART:
  Oh – nothing much. The other night, insomnia
  Tormented me, and two or three ideas
  Entered my head. Today I wrote them down.
  I'd like to hear what you think. Some other time.
  You're not in the mood for me today.

SALIERI: Ah! Mozart!
  Mozart! When am I not in the mood for you?
  Sit down. I'm listening.

MOZART [*at the piano*]:   All right. Imagine . . .
  Who? Well, say myself – a little younger;
  In love, but not too much; only a little;
  I'm with a pretty woman, or a friend,
  Say you; I'm feeling merry . . . Suddenly

151

A vision of the grave, that sudden darkness;
Something like that, perhaps . . . Anyway, listen.

[*Plays.*]

SALIERI:

You were coming to me with this, and you could stop
To hear a blind fiddler at an inn? My God, Mozart,
You are not worthy of yourself.

MOZART: Is it good?

SALIERI:

What depth! What daring and what harmony!
You are a god, Mozart, and do not know it.
I know it.

MOZART: Bah! Really? . . . Maybe you're right.
But my godhead's starving.

SALIERI: Then, let's dine together
At the Golden Lion.

MOZART: I'd love to. But just let
Me run home to tell my wife not to expect me
For dinner.

SALIERI: All right, but make sure you come back.
I'll wait for you . . . No! I can't resist
My fate: I am chosen to stop him —
Otherwise we are all finished, all
Of us priests and servants of music,
Not merely I with my dim glory . . .
What good will be served if Mozart lives
And scales yet greater heights? Will he raise
Art thereby? No! It will fall again

When he goes: he will leave us no heir.
What good does he do? Like some cherub
He has brought a few heavenly songs
Only to fly away after he's stirred
A wingless desire in us
Children of dust! So, fly away then!
The sooner the better! For eighteen
Years I have carried about with me
This poison, Isora's last gift –
And often, I've sat at the table
With my carefree foe, thinking my life
An intolerable torment; yet
Never have I yielded to the whisper
Of temptation, though I am
No coward, though I feel the deep wrong
Done to me, though I have little love
For life. I've always bided my time.
When the thirst for death tormented me,
I would think: 'Why die? Perhaps life still
Has unexpected gifts to offer;
Perhaps rapture will visit me,
The creative night and inspiration;
Perhaps a new Haydn will create
Great things and I shall enjoy them . . .' When
I dined with a hated guest, I used
To think: 'Perhaps I shall find a still
More loathsome companion; perhaps some
Mountainous hurt will crash upon me
From a lordly height – then you will not
Come amiss, O gift of Isora!'
And I was right! At last I have found
My enemy, and a new Haydn
Has enraptured me with ecstasy!
Now is the time; O sacred gift of love,
Dissolve in the cup of friendship!

Private room at an inn; piano; MOZART *and* SALIERI *at table.*

SALIERI:

Why are you gloomy today?

MOZART: I? Not at all!

SALIERI:

You are worried by something, Mozart, I feel sure.
Good dinner – fine wine – but you are silent, glum.

MOZART:

I confess my *Requiem* is worrying me.

SALIERI:

Ah! You're writing a *Requiem*?

MOZART: Yes, but a strange
Occurrence . . . Didn't I tell you about it?

SALIERI: No.

MOZART:

Well, about three weeks ago I came home late.
I was told someone had called to see me. Why,
I don't know, but all that night I thought:
Who was it? And what does he want of me?
The next day, he called again, the same man; and
Again I happened to be out. On the third day,
While I was playing with my little boy
In the nursery, the stranger was announced.
He was dressed in black. Courteously bowing,
He commissioned a *Requiem*, and vanished. I
Immediately sat down and began to write.

154

I have not seen him since; yet I am glad:
Although the *Requiem* is ready, I'd
Be loath to part with it. But all the same . . .

SALIERI:
  What?

MOZART:
      I am ashamed to admit to such a thing.

SALIERI:
  Admit what?

MOZART: Day and night my man in black
  Gives me no rest. He haunts me everywhere
  Like a shadow. And even now he seems
  To be sitting here with the two of us.

SALIERI: Enough!
  Mozart, this is childish superstition.
  Throw it off. Beaumarchais used to say:
  'Salieri, my brother, when you have black thoughts,
  Either uncork a bottle of champagne,
  Or else re-read *The Marriage of Figaro*!'

MOZART:
  Ah yes! Beaumarchais was a friend of yours—
  You wrote *Tarare* for him, a glorious piece.
  There's one tune in it that I always whistle
  When I'm feeling happy . . . La-la, la-la . . .
  Wonderful tune! . . . Salieri, is it true
  Beaumarchais poisoned someone once?

SALIERI: I doubt it:
  He was too humorous for such a trade.

MOZART:
　　I'm glad. He was a genius, like you and me.
　　Genius and villainy are incompatible,
　　Don't you agree?

SALIERI:　　　　　　　You think so?

　　　[*Casts the poison into* MOZART's *glass*]

　　　　　　　　　　Come, drink up!

MOZART:
　　Your health, my friend! Let's drink to the true bond
　　Linking us two sons of harmony.

　　　　　　[*Drinks.*]

SALIERI:
　　Wait, wait, wait! You've drunk it . . . without me?

MOZART [*throwing his napkin on the table*]:
　　Enough. I've had my fill.

　　　　　[*Goes to the piano.*]

　　　　　　　　　Now, listen, Salieri,
　　To my *Requiem*.

　　　　　　[*Plays.*]

　　　You're crying.

SALIERI:　　　　　　　　　I shed these tears
　　For the first time: I feel both pain and pleasure,
　　As though I had cut off some suffering limb.
　　Mozart, my friend, these tears . . . pay no attention.
　　Fill my soul with those enchanting sounds . . .

MOZART:

    If everyone felt as deeply as you the power
    Of harmony! Yet no: for then the world
    Could not even exist; there would be no one
    To care for the needs of ordinary life
    – All would surrender themselves to the freedom of art.
    There have to be just a few of us, I fear,
    Chosen to be idle and happy, and to play,
    Without thought of being useful; priests of beauty.
    Isn't that so? But I'm not well today.
    Something has disagreed with me. I'll go
    And have a sleep. Farewell.

SALIERI: Till we meet again.

            [*Alone.*]

    You will sleep long, Mozart! But can it be
    That he is right, and I am not a genius?
    Genius and villainy are incompatible . . .
    It's not true: think of Michelangelo.
    Or is that a fiction of the senseless rabble?
    Was the Vatican's builder not a murderer?

                            [1830]

THE STONE GUEST

LEPORELLO:

O statua gentilissima
Del gran Commendatore! . . .
Ah, Padrone!

Don Giovanni

SCENE I

DON JUAN *and* LEPORELLO

DON JUAN:

W<small>E'LL</small> wait here until night. Madrid again!
Soon I'll be flitting through familiar lanes,
Cloaked, and my hat pulled down over my eyes —
I'm hardly likely to be recognized:
Agreed?

LEPORELLO:

Agreed! Since every other knave
Will look like him, Don Juan will be safe!

DON JUAN:

You're mocking me! Who'll know me, then, tonight?

LEPORELLO:

Why, only the first watchman that you meet,
Gypsy or fiddler, reeling in the street,
Or one of your own kind, some renegade
With flowing cloak, dying to draw his blade.

DON JUAN:

Suppose I'm recognized, what do I care?
In all Madrid there's no one whom I fear,
Except the king.

LEPORELLO: And tomorrow he will hear
  Don Juan has been seen within the city,
  Breaking his term of exile. What will he
  Do then, do you think?

DON JUAN: Condemn me to the block,
  Unquestionably! No, he'll just send me back.
  I haven't broken any of his laws.
  He exiled me in charity because
  I was being plagued to death by those deranged
  Relations of the dead man.

LEPORELLO: – Who won't have changed.
  We should have stayed; we led a pleasant life.

DON JUAN:
  Oh, you've decided that! I nearly died
  Of boredom there. God, what a place! The sky
  A pall of smoke. The women? Why, I swear
  – My foolish Leporello – I prefer
  The poorest girl in Andalusia to
  The finest beauties I found there. It's true!
  Oh, I confess, at first they took me in,
  Their modesty, their blue eyes, their white skin;
  Above all, their novelty; but, thank the Lord,
  I quickly had the good sense to get bored
  With them – gazing at those vapid creatures,
  Those wax dolls, with their lifeless, empty features;
  Whereas our girls! . . . But wait! I recognize
  This place, I'm sure I do.

LEPORELLO: I'm not surprised:
  It is the Convent of St Anthony.
  We've spent time here – you, more agreeably
  Than I. I held the horses in this grove,
  I don't know what you held.

DON JUAN [*pensively*]:   Inez, my love!
    My poor Inez . . . cold in the grave!

LEPORELLO: The black-
    Eyed girl? Ah yes! For three months you attacked
    Her walls in vain, till the Devil let you graze.

DON JUAN:
    July it was . . . at night . . . My poor Inez.
    Strange, how I loved her melancholy gaze,
    Her lips that were as pale as ash. You thought
    Her plain, I recall. And truly, she was not
    Beautiful in any real sense.
    Only her eyes, her eyes . . . and such a glance
    Came flashing from them, under those heavy lids . . .
    And then, her voice, soft, like an invalid's . . .
    I didn't know how cruel her husband was
    Until it was too late . . . My poor Inez!

LEPORELLO:
    Yet quickly on her heels came others.

DON JUAN: Yes.

LEPORELLO:
    Still others, if we live.

DON JUAN: I can't deny it.

LEPORELLO:
    And now, what tasty morsel for your diet
    Have you a mind for in Madrid?

DON JUAN: Why, who
    But Laura? We must go.

LEPORELLO: I'll follow you.

DON JUAN:

With her, the bold approach was always best.
If she's got someone with her, I'll suggest
He exit hurriedly through the window.

LEPORELLO: Good!
That's talking! I didn't think a dead girl could
Disturb our spirits for long. Who's drawing near,
Gliding between graves?

[*Enter* MONK.]

MONK: Soon she will be here.
. . . Who's this? Servants of Donna Anna?

LEPORELLO: We're
Our own masters.

DON JUAN: You were expecting – whom?

MONK:

Donna Anna to her husband's tomb;
Her nightly visitation.

DON JUAN: Donna Anna
Da Solva? What? The wife of the commander
Who was killed by – I can't recall his name?

MONK:

Vile, dissolute Don Juan.

LEPORELLO: Oh! his fame
Has even reached the convent now! By nuns
And anchorites his eulogies are sung!

161

MONK:
Perhaps you know him?

LEPORELLO: We? No. God forbid.
Where is he to be found?

MONK: Not in Madrid.
In exile, far away.

LEPORELLO: They should be racked,
Such rogues, or bundled all into one sack,
And flung into the sea. Exile's too kind.

DON JUAN:
What foolery –

LEPORELLO: Quiet! It's just a blind.

DON JUAN:
So it is here the lady's husband sleeps?

MONK:
Just here. And every day she comes and weeps
Before his monument, praying her Saviour
To grant him peace.

DON JUAN: What curious behaviour
For a widow! Is she pretty?

MONK: It's a sin
For us monks to be moved by feminine
Beauty; but it is sinful, too, to lie.
St Anthony himself would not deny
She's wonderfully beautiful.

DON JUAN: So he
    – The dead man – had good cause for jealousy.
    He kept her locked away, it would appear:
    Dead to the world. I'd like to talk to her.

MONK:
    Oh, Donna Anna never talks with men.

DON JUAN:
    Except with you, good father – now and then?

MONK:
    I'm just a harmless monk; that's different.
    There is the lady.

            [*Enter* DONNA ANNA.]

DONNA ANNA: Open the monument,
    Good holy father.

MONK: At once, Señora.

            [DONNA ANNA *follows the* MONK.]

LEPORELLO: Well,
    What is she like?

DON JUAN: There's nothing visible
    Of her beneath her sombre veil; I caught
    Only a fleeting vision of her foot
    – Trim little heel.

LEPORELLO: That's quite enough for you.
    Your fantasy will open to your view
    The whole of her immediately. Your lush
    Imagination's like the painter's brush;

No matter where you start, the rest will follow
By instinct – arms, thighs, breasts . . .

DON JUAN: O Leporello,
   I'll get to know her.

LEPORELLO: There he goes! The man's
   A wonder; having killed the husband, plans
   To bathe in the widow's tears! That's going too far,
   Even for such a wretch.

DON JUAN: There's the first star.
   Let's take advantage of brief night. The moon
   Will change it to a glowing twilight soon.
   Let's creep into Madrid.

                    [*He leaves.*]

LEPORELLO: Like any thief
   He greets the shades of darkness with relief
   – And fears the moon. God, what a life! A curse!
   My strength gives way. The grave could not be worse.

SCENE II

Room. Supper at LAURA'*s.*

FIRST GUEST:
   Laura, I've never seen you pour your soul
   Quite so profoundly into any role.
   Tonight, my dear, you *were* the character.

164

SECOND GUEST:
  You drew a world of meaning out of her.
  Such power!

THIRD GUEST: Such art!

LAURA: Well, yes, I do admit
  Today I felt I was inspired in it;
  As though myself were lost within the part;
  As though not feeble memory, but the heart
  Gave birth to words and movements . . .

FIRST GUEST: And your eyes
  Shine still, your cheeks still glow, your ecstasy's
  Not faded yet. We'll not allow it to
  Grow cold before we hear a song from you.
  Please, Laura, sing us something.

LAURA: Give me my
  Guitar.

                [*Sings.*]

ALL: Ah! Bravo!

FIRST GUEST: Thank you. Your melody
  Has cast enchantment over us. Among
  The joys of life, to love alone does song
  Yield up the prize. Yet, when you're singing, love
  And song are one . . . Behold, you even move
  Carlos, your surly guest! He's touched!

SECOND GUEST: Such chords!
  There's so much soul in them! Who wrote the words,
  Laura?

LAURA: Don Juan.

DON CARLOS: What! Don Juan?

LAURA: He.
My true friend and false love wrote them for me.

DON CARLOS:
Don Juan is a wicked, godless knave;
And you – are a fool.

LAURA: Are you mad? I'll have
My servants kill you for that – your rank won't save
You, Spaniard!

DON CARLOS [*stands*]:
Call them, then.

FIRST GUEST: No, Laura, no;
Calm yourself, please. Don Carlos, let it go;
Sit down. She has forgotten . . .

LAURA: What? That Don Juan
Killed his brother honourably in a duel?
I wish he'd killed *him* too.

DON CARLOS: I'm sorry. It
Was stupid of me to get angry.

LAURA: You admit
Your stupidity? Well then, our quarrel's done.

DON CARLOS:
Forgive me, Laura. I lose my senses when
I hear that name. You ought to know that.

LAURA: I
Can't help it if his name instinctively
Springs to my lips.

GUEST: Come, as a sign that you're
No longer angry, Laura, sing once more
For us.

LAURA: All right; a goodnight song. What shall
I sing? Ah! listen! . . .

[*She sings.*]

ALL: Charming! Wonderful!

LAURA:
Good night, my friends.

GUESTS: Thank you and good night,
Laura.

[*They go out.* LAURA *stops* DON CARLOS]

LAURA: You, madman! Stay awhile. I like
You. You reminded me of Don Juan. He'd
Grind his teeth like that, abusing me.

DON CARLOS:
You loved him?

[LAURA *nods.*]

Deeply?

[*She nods again.*]

                    Lucky man! And do
You love him still?

167

LAURA: Not while I'm here with you.
    I can't love two men. Now I love you.

DON CARLOS: Laura,
    How old are you?

LAURA: Eighteen.

DON CARLOS: You're young . . . and for
    Five or six years more you will be young.
    For six years more you'll have a faithful throng
    Around you, flattering, seeking to persuade
    You to grant them favours; nightly serenades
    Will entertain you; at dawn, in quiet glades,
    Young men will kill each other for your love.
    But when your prime has passed, the sparkle of
    Your eyes grown dim, dark shadows under them,
    When grey hairs gleam among the black, and men
    Already speak of you as old – what then?

LAURA:
    Ah, then . . . but why be thinking now of that?
    Or do you always have such thoughts? Come out
    On to the balcony. How calm the sky;
    The air is warm and does not stir, the night
    With lemon and with laurel breathes, the moon
    Is shining brightly in the dense, dark blue,
    The watchman's drawn-out cry resounds: 'All's well! . . .'
    But far away now in the north – in Paris –
    Perhaps the sky is overcast with clouds,
    A cold rain's falling and the wind is blowing,
    But what is that to us? Now listen, Carlos,
    I order you to smile at me . . . That's right!

DON CARLOS:
Enchanting demon!

[*Knock at the door.*]

DON JUAN: Laura, ho!

LAURA: Who's there?
Whose voice is that? It sounds –

DON JUAN: Unlock the door . . .

LAURA:
Lord! can it be? . . .

[*Opens the door. Enter* DON JUAN.]

DON JUAN: Good evening!

LAURA: Juan! . . .

[LAURA *throws herself on his neck.*]

DON CARLOS: What!
Don Juan! . . .

DON JUAN: Laura, my dearest!   [*Kisses her*]
                              But who is that?

DON CARLOS:
It's I. Don Carlos.

DON JUAN: An unexpected pleasure!
Tomorrow morning I shall be at leisure
To answer you.

DON CARLOS: No! Now – at once.

LAURA: Don Carlos,
I beg you to recall you're in my house,
Not in the street. Please go away.

DON CARLOS: I'm waiting.
Your sword is at your side.

DON JUAN: If you're impatient,
Very well.

                    [*They fight.*]

LAURA: Oh! Oh! Juan! . . .

        [*Throws herself on the bed.* DON CARLOS *falls.*]

DON JUAN: Laura, get up,
It's over.

LAURA: What, is he dead? Oh marvellous!
Dead in my house! What shall I do now?
Villain, devil, perhaps you'll tell me how
I'm to dispose of him?

DON JUAN: Maybe he's still
Living.

LAURA: Oh yes, still living! Look, you devil.
You've pierced him through the heart – you never fail.
A small three-cornered wound, a mere love-bite,
But enough – no blood, no breath.

DON JUAN: He asked for it.

LAURA:
Ah, Juan, you vex me! You haven't changed one bit.
Always the other fellow's in the wrong! . . .
Where have you come from? Have you been here long?

DON JUAN:
I've only just arrived – in secret, for
I've not been pardoned.

LAURA: And you thought of your
Laura at once?

DON JUAN: And came.

LAURA: Well, that was sweet.
I don't believe you. You were passing in the street
And saw my house. You're such a lying fellow.

DON JUAN:
No, Laura. Ask my servant, Leporello.
I've put up in a wretched inn outside
The city. I've risked stealing through Madrid
For Laura's sake.

                    [*He kisses her.*]

LAURA: Oh darling . . . I've longed for you . . .
No, stop! In front of *him*! What *shall* we do
With him?

DON JUAN: Just let him sleep. Before daybreak
I'll drag him from the house, wrapped in my cloak,
And dump him at the crossroads.

LAURA: Only make sure
Nobody sees you. It was lucky your
Visit was not a moment sooner. I'd
Been entertaining friends to supper. They'd
Only just left.

DON JUAN: How long have you loved him?

LAURA: Who?
You must be crazy.

DON JUAN: How many times have you
Made love while I've been gone, you little tramp?
I want the truth!

LAURA: What about you, you scamp?

DON JUAN:
Tell me . . . No, later . . .

SCENE III

The Commander's Monument.

DON JUAN:
All's for the best: an unintended stroke
Killing Don Carlos, I'm here in a monk's cloak
Hiding – where at every dusk I see
My charming widow. I think she's noticed me.
Our greetings have been formal, but today
I'll break the ice. How, though? 'Señora, may
I presume . . .?' Or no – 'May I be so bold . . .?'
Best, like a love song, allow it to unfold
Extempore. She should be here. The old

Commander's bored, I guess, without her. He's
Built like a giant, a very Hercules . . .
Bull-like shoulders . . . How tall and powerful
They've made his statue, whereas he was small,
Puny even. If he stretched up on his toes
He might perhaps have reached his statue's nose.
That day when on my rapier-point he ran,
He perished like a dragonfly on a pin.
But he was tough – a proud and valiant man.
Ah! there she is at last.

[*Enter* DONNA ANNA.]

DONNA ANNA: He's here again.
  O Father, forgive me for distracting you
  From holy meditation.

DON JUAN: It's I who
  Should beg your pardon, Señora; for I know
  A stranger's presence can impede the flow
  Of sorrow.

DONNA ANNA:
        No. I sorrow inwardly;
  And in your presence my humble prayers will fly
  More swiftly up to heaven. Pray with me,
  Father.

DON JUAN:
        I, pray with you, Donna Anna! I!
  Oh no, I could not. My lips are too impure
  For such a happiness. I'd never dare
  Repeat your supplications. From afar
  I must observe you when, in silence, you
  Spread out your raven tresses on the tomb's

Pale marble. Then it seems that secretly
An angel has alighted. Then, in me,
I find no prayers, but only speechless wonder,
And in my heart I think—happy commander,
Whose tomb is warmed by her celestial breath,
Freshened by her tears . . . O enviable death!

DONNA ANNA:
These are strange words . . .

DON JUAN: Señora?

DONNA ANNA: . . . to a lonely
Woman . . . You have forgotten . . .

DON JUAN: That I'm only
A wretched hermit? That my sinful voice
Should not resound so loudly in this place?

DONNA ANNA:
I thought . . . You seemed . . . But I apologize
If I've . . .

DON JUAN: Aha! You've seen through my disguise!

DONNA ANNA:
Good holy Father, I don't understand.

DON JUAN:
You've seen that I'm no monk. I kneel down and
Humbly implore your pardon.

DONNA ANNA: O heavens! Get up,
Get up . . . Who are you?

DON JUAN: Of a hopeless love
The wretched victim.

DONNA ANNA: O God, before his grave!
Leave me at once.

DON JUAN: A minute, Donna Anna,
Only a single minute – on my honour!

DONNA ANNA:
If someone comes! . . .

DON JUAN: The gate is locked.

DONNA ANNA: Well? Speak.
What is your wish?

DON JUAN: To die here at your feet.
I'd wish my poor dust to be buried here,
Not mixed with the dust of him who is so dear
To you – not here – not close – farther away,
Over there, at the entrance, by the gates,
Where with your light step or your garment's hem
You might brush past my gravestone when you come
This way at dusk to spread your tresses on
This tomb and weep.

DONNA ANNA: Your mind is surely gone.

DON JUAN:
Is it a sign of madness to want death?
Madness is wanting life, when every breath
Is tortured, hopeless longing that one day
I'd move your heart to tender love. Were I
A madman, I would spend the nights below

Your window, singing; go everywhere you go,
Always in your sight and hearing, not
Hiding from you in this accursed spot,
Suffering in silence . . .

DONNA ANNA: You call this silence?

DON JUAN: Chance,
Donna Anna, carried me away. *Mis*chance;
For otherwise you never would have wrung
My secret from me.

DONNA ANNA: Have you loved me long?

DON JUAN:
Long have I loved you, or not long? I can
But say there came an hour when life began
To seem, though transitory, not absurd,
And happiness no longer just a word.

DONNA ANNA:
Leave me, I pray; you are a dangerous man.

DON JUAN:
Dangerous? How?

DONNA ANNA: I fear to listen.

DON JUAN: Then,
I'll be silent, locked in holy contemplation.
Don't send me away. My only consolation
Is seeing you. I ask, I hope, I seek
Nothing to bring a blush into your cheeks;
But if I *must* live, I must see you.

DONNA ANNA: Please

    Go. This is not the place for words like these,
    For madness such as this. Tomorrow you
    May visit me at home; if you swear to
    Preserve an honourable and fitting distance,
    I'll receive you, in the evening, later, – since
    My husband died, I have seen no one.

DON JUAN: O

    Donna Anna! – Angel! God comfort you,
    As you have comforted this sufferer.

DONNA ANNA:

    Now go at once.

DON JUAN: I pray, one minute more.

DONNA ANNA:

    Then *I* must go. My mind is far from prayer.
    Your worldly speeches have distracted me;
    I am not used to them . . . have never been
    Used to them. Tomorrow, I shall receive
    You.

DON JUAN:

    Yes! And even now I can't believe,
    Can't trust, my happiness . . . Tomorrow
    I'll see you! – not here, not by stealth!

DONNA ANNA: Tomorrow,

    Yes, tomorrow. What is your name?

DON JUAN: Diego

    De Calvado.

DONNA ANNA: Farewell, Don Diego.

[*She leaves*]

DON JUAN: Leporello!

[*Enter* LEPORELLO.]

LEPORELLO:
  What do you want?

DON JUAN: Dear friend! What bliss! 'Tomorrow
  In the evening, later . . .' My Leporello,
  Tomorrow! I'm happy as a child! . . . Be
  Prepared . . .

LEPORELLO: So you've spoken to the lady? She
  Has graced you with a pleasant word or two,
  Or you bestowed on her your blessing.

DON JUAN: No,
  Leporello, no! An assignation!
  The lady granted me an assignation!

LEPORELLO:
  O widows, you are all alike; your rings
  Are frail as thread.

DON JUAN: I'm so happy, I could sing,
  Or embrace the world!

LEPORELLO: But what about the commander?
  What's he going to say?

DON JUAN: Our marble pander?
  Oh, he's all right; an understanding man;
  And he's grown meeker since his death began.

LEPORELLO:
No; look at his statue.

DON JUAN: Well?

LEPORELLO: It looks as though
It's gazing angrily at you.

DON JUAN: Then, go
And ask it if it would like to visit us
Tomorrow – I mean, at Donna Anna's house.

LEPORELLO:
Invite the statue! Why?

DON JUAN: Not to converse.
Ask it to come to Donna Anna's house
Tomorrow, at a late hour – after dark –
To guard the door.

LEPORELLO: That's an odd kind of joke,
And at whose expense?

DON JUAN: Do it.

LEPORELLO: But . . .

DON JUAN: Go on.

LEPORELLO:
Pre-eminent and beautiful statue, Don
Juan, my master, invites you to your wife's house
Tomorrow evening, at a late hour . . .
O Lord, I am afraid; I cannot.

DON JUAN: Coward!
   Do as I say, or else . . .

LEPORELLO: All right, all right.
   My master bids you come tomorrow night
   To the house of your widow, at a late hour,
   And guard the door . . .

                  [*The* STATUE *nods.*]

                         Ai!

DON JUAN: What's the matter now?

LEPORELLO:
   Ai, ai! . . . Ai, ai . . .

DON JUAN: What's wrong?

LEPORELLO [*nodding*]:   The statue . . . ai!

DON JUAN:
   You're bowing!

LEPORELLO: No, not I – but it! I'll die!

DON JUAN:
   What stupid nonsense!

LEPORELLO: All right, *you* talk to it.

DON JUAN:
   I will, you rogue. [*To the* STATUE.]
                  Commander, I invite
   You to your widow's house, tomorrow night,

When Donna Anna and I will be at home,
To stand guard at the doors for us. You'll come?
                    [*The* STATUE *nods again.*]
Oh God!

LEPORELLO:

      I told you . . .

DON JUAN: Let's get out of here.

SCENE IV

DONNA ANNA's *Room.* DON JUAN *and* DONNA ANNA

DONNA ANNA:
I have received you, Don Diego, but
I fear my gloom is making you regret
Your visit. Poor widow as I am, I see
The lost one everywhere about me. I
Am weeping when I smile, like April. Why
Are you silent?

DON JUAN: I am enjoying silently
And deeply the thought that I'm alone with you,
Donna Anna. Not at the monument to
That fortunate dead man, your marble spouse,
Seeing you kneel before him: but here, in your house.

DONNA ANNA:
You're jealous of my husband? In his tomb?
He tortures you, Don Diego?

DON JUAN: I ought not to
Be jealous. He was your choice.

DONNA ANNA: Oh no! My mother
Chose to bind our hands and hearts together,
For Don Alvaro was rich and we were poor.

DON JUAN:
Lucky Don Alvaro! He laid before
The feet of a goddess nothing but empty treasures,
And got in return all paradise's pleasures.
If I had known you first, I'd have bestowed
On you my rank, my wealth, and everything I owned,
Just for a single, gentle glance; devoted
Slave to you, night and day, I should have noted
All your desires, to anticipate them, and
So make your life an enchantment without end.
Alas! Quite otherwise did fate decree.

DONNA ANNA:
Ah, Diego, stop: it is a sin for me
To listen to such words – I cannot love
You; a widow must stay faithful to the grave.
Oh, if you only knew how Don Alvaro
Loved me! If I had died first, Don Alvaro
Would never have received into his home
– Never – a lady who was in love with him.
He would have remained constant to his vows.

DON JUAN:
This everlasting harping on your spouse
Tortures my heart, Donna Anna. You've punished me
Enough for one day, though I deserved to be
Punished, I know.

DONNA ANNA: Why punished? You're not linked
By holy bond to anyone, I think?
In loving me, therefore, you do no wrong
Either towards heaven, or me.

DON JUAN: Towards you! O God!

DONNA ANNA:
It isn't possible you're guilty of
Any wrong towards me. Or, tell me, how?

DON JUAN:
No! No, never.

DONNA ANNA: Diego, I must know
If you have wronged me. Speak.

DON JUAN: Not for the world.

DONNA ANNA:
If there is any wrongdoing, I must be told.

DON JUAN:
No, no!

DONNA ANNA:
          What was it you said to me just now?
You'd be my devoted slave? So this is how
You'd serve my every desire! Diego, I
Am getting angry. Answer! Tell me why
You think you've wronged me.

DON JUAN: I dare not tell you, for
You would hate me.

DONNA ANNA: No, I pardon you before
I know the offence. Don Diego, I implore
You, I demand, that you tell me . . .

DON JUAN: Don't seek to know
The terrible, mortal secret.

DONNA ANNA: Mortal! . . . Oh
Diego, you're torturing me. What *is* it? How
Can a stranger such as you have wronged a lonely
Woman? I have no enemies. The only
One I can think of is the man who killed
My husband.

DON JUAN [*to himself*]:
The dénouement approaches! – Did
You know Don Juan?

DONNA ANNA: I've never seen him.

DON JUAN: But
You nurse against him an implacable hate?

DONNA ANNA:
As honour binds me. But you're trying to
Divert me from the subject, Don Diego –
I insist you tell me . . .

DON JUAN: Supposing you should meet
Don Juan?

DONNA ANNA:
I'd stab the villain in the heart.

DON JUAN:
Where is your dagger, Donna Anna? Here is my heart.

DONNA ANNA:
Diego, what are you saying?

DON JUAN: Not Diego, I'm
Juan.

DONNA ANNA:

    O God! No, it cannot be, I
Don't believe you.

DON JUAN: I'm Don Juan.

DONNA ANNA: It's not true.

DON JUAN:

I'm afraid it is; I ran your husband through;
I don't regret it – there's no remorse in me.

DONNA ANNA:

What am I hearing? No, no, it cannot be.

DON JUAN:

I'm Don Juan and I love you.

DONNA ANNA [*falling*]:   Where am I? Where?
I feel ill . . . ill.

DON JUAN: Heavens! What's happened to her?
What's wrong with you, Donna Anna? Get up,
Get up, pull yourself together, wake up;
Your slave is at your feet, your Diego.

DONNA ANNA: Leave
Me! [*Weakly.*] O my enemy. You have taken from me
Everything I had in life . . .

DON JUAN: Dearest creature,
I'll expiate. I'm waiting at your feet for
Your command, to die, or else to breathe for you
Alone . . .

DONNA ANNA:
>So this is Don Juan . . .

DON JUAN: Isn't it true
He's been described to you as a monster? O
Donna Anna, the rumour does not lie; a load
Of evils weigh on my weary conscience; I
Have always been an adept in lechery;
But from the moment when I first saw you,
Everything has changed; I have been born anew,
Or so it seems to me. For, loving you,
Virtue herself I love, and for the first
Time ever, it is for virtue that I thirst,
And I kneel humbly before you, as at a well
Of pure water.

DONNA ANNA: O you are eloquent in evil,
I've heard; a sly seducer, the very devil
In a handsome form. How many poor women have
You destroyed?

DON JUAN: Till now, not one of them did I love.

DONNA ANNA:
And now, Don Juan's in love for the first time,
And doesn't see me as a victim! I'm
To believe that?

DON JUAN: It's hard. But if I'd wanted to
Deceive you, would I have confessed the truth,
Uttering the name you can't endure? Is this
Another instance of my wickedness?

DONNA ANNA:
Who knows? Who knows you? But how could you come
So brazenly tonight into my home
Where every moment might bring death to you?

DON JUAN:
What's death? For one sweet moment's tryst, I'd throw
My life away without regret.

DONNA ANNA: But how,
You reckless man, are we to get you out
Of here unseen?

DON JUAN [*kissing her hand*]:
                    So you're concerned about
Poor Juan's life! Then in your heavenly soul
There is no hatred, Donna Anna?

DONNA ANNA: Oh,
If only I could hate you! But you must leave.

DON JUAN:
When shall we meet again?

DONNA ANNA: I don't believe
We should . . . Not soon.

DON JUAN: Not till – tomorrow night?

DONNA ANNA:
Where?

DON JUAN:
           Here.

DONNA ANNA: O Don Juan, how weak is this heart
  Of mine.

DON JUAN: In sign of forgiveness, a quiet kiss?

DONNA ANNA:
  No, please go.

DON JUAN: One cold, quiet . . .

DONNA ANNA: Ah, you press
  Too hard, too hard! Well, there. Oh God, there's someone
  Knocking . . . Quick, hide, Don Juan.

DON JUAN: Goodbye, until
  We meet again, my love. [*Goes out and runs in again.*]
                Ah! . . .

DONNA ANNA: What's the matter?
  Ah! . . .

  [*Enter the* STATUE *of the Commander.* DONNA ANNA *falls.*]

STATUE:
        I've come as you asked.

DON JUAN: O God! Donna Anna!

STATUE:
  Don't touch her, all's over. You're trembling, Don Juan.

DON JUAN:
  I? no, not at all. I invited you; I knew you'd
  Try to come.

STATUE: Give me your hand.

188

DON JUAN   My pleasure . . .
   O how cold and heavy is the pressure
   Of his stone hand! Release me – let go my hand . . .
   I'm perishing – all's over – O Donna Anna!

              [*They sink into the ground*]

                                    [1830]

189

THE TALE OF TSAR SALTAN

of his son, the famed and mighty hero
Duke Guidon Saltanovich
and of the passing fair Princess Swan

THREE sisters as the day grew cool
Sat by a window spinning wool.
'If I were Queen,' said one of them,
'I'd feast the whole of Christendom.'
'If I were Queen,' her sister smiled,
'I would make clothes for all the world.'
Spoke the third girl: 'If I were Queen,
I'd bear our King a noble son.'

Scarcely had she finished speaking
Than the door gave a gentle creak and
Into the chamber comes the King.
He'd overheard their chattering
As he passed by the house. The last
Speech was the one that pleased him most.
'Hail, fair Queen!' he smiled. 'Remember,
I'd like a son before September.
Yes, yes, be Queen! And as for you
– Sisters, little doves – come too.
Do follow us. No need to live here.
One can be cook, and one our weaver.'

Off to the palace they trooped together
Behind that fair land's King and Father.
Not being one who liked delay,
He had the wedding that same day.
King Saltan at the feast that night
Sat with the Queen upon his right;
And then the guests of honour led

The young couple to an ivory bed.
Cook in the kitchen is full of gloom
And weeps the weaver at the loom,
In envy of the Queen, who smiled,
And bore, from that first night, a child.

Just at that time, a war began.
Mounting his charger, King Saltán
Made sad farewells, implored his wife,
As she loved him, to guard her life,
And galloped off to join the fray.
While he was fighting far away,
The Queen has had a son – a strong
And handsome baby, a yard long;
He was as warm upon her breast
As the young eaglet in the nest;
A messenger went off galloping
To take the good news to the King.
But the weaver and the cook,
With the crone – old Babarook –
Muttered together and agreed
To have the messenger waylaid;
And sent another in his place,
Bearing a letter that said this:
'The Queen this very night has borne
Not a daughter nor a son;
Not a frog, and not a mouse,
But something quite mysterious.'

When the Father King had heard
The horrid message word for word,
In his wrath he raved and ranted,
Ordered the herald hanged; relented;
Sent back home this message: 'Do
Nothing till I come to you.'

With this letter in his pack
The messenger at length got back.
But the weaver and the cook,
With the crone, old Babarook,
Take him aside, ply him with drink;
Into a drowse they watch him sink,
Then slip into his pouch of leather
A different message altogether –
And the drunk herald later brought
The following order to the court:
'The King commands his court today
Not to brook any more delay;
The Queen's to be cast secretly,
With what she's borne, into the sea.'
They thought a wound had made him mad,
Grieved for their Queen, and for the lad.
It seemed a dreadful sin – but still . . .
They thronged in, told her the King's will –
For her and her son, ill destiny,
Read out the sovereign's decree,
And put them both, that very hour,
Into a barrel caulked with tar,
Sailed far out, rolled it in the water –
And washed their hands of the sad matter.

In dark-blue sky the stars abound,
In dark-blue sea waves plash them round;
Cloud wipes the stars out like a rag,
Over the dim sea swims the keg.
The Queen is weeping, struggling, in it,
But the child's growing by the minute.
The Queen is going mad – she raves . . .
But her babe cries to the waves: 'You, waves,
My waves! you play about, you're free,
You roam wherever you want to be,

You lift a ship, or flood an island –
Save us! Wash us on to dry land!
Don't let us die!' The waves obeyed,
Washed them inshore, and gently laid
The keg down and plashed off again.
They're saved, the mother and her son;
She feels a beach, without a doubt.
But what's the good? Who'll let them out?
Unless God takes a hand, they're dead.
The child rose, placed his tiny head
Against the wood, and took the strain.
'Why don't we break a window-pane
Through to outside?' he said, and burst
The bottom out – flew out head first.

Mother and son are safe and sound;
On barren heath they see a mound,
All around is dark-blue sea,
Upon the mound a green oak-tree.
The son thought, gazing at it – good,
We're both in need of tasty food.
He made a stout bow from the oak
By bending-in the branch he broke,
From his crucifix he now
Rips the silk cord to string the bow,
A tender little shoot broke off
To make an arrow sharp enough
To pierce a rabbit or a hare,
And wandered off along the shore.

Tracing the highwater-mark
He thinks he hears a groaning – hark!
All is not quiet in the sea!
A swan is struggling dreadfully
Amid the waves – above, a kite,

A bird of prey, is poised in flight
Ready to plunge down at the poor
Creature – the more she strives, the more
She's dragged down in the churning water . . .
The kite is ready for the slaughter,
Its beak is whetted, talons spread . . .
But all at once the arrow sped
Striking the kite unerringly –
The kite spilled blood into the sea,
A moment later, the kite is down,
Threshing in the sea, will drown;
It groans with an unbirdlike cry;
The swan, now drifting safe nearby,
Pecks at it, beats it with her wing,
Speeds the black creature's perishing –
It's drowned. The swan turns to the beach
And speaks to the Prince in Russian speech:
'You, Prince, my saviour, do not grieve
Because you are condemned to starve
For three whole days because of me;
Truly, your arrow's lost at sea,
Truly, the sea has drunk your arrow;
This sorrow – it is not a sorrow.
With all good things I shall repay you,
Serve you hereafter and obey you:
You see, it is no swan you save,
A maiden you have kept alive;
You have not shot a bird of prey,
A warlock has been killed today.
I shan't forget you, Prince, I swear:
You will find me everywhere,
Remember what the swan has said.
Go back now. Fret not. Go to bed.'

The swan flew off across the deep,
The Prince and Queen went off to sleep
With hunger pangs. And now he wakes;
The fancies of the night he shakes
Off, because a new surprise
Awaits the Prince: before his eyes
Stands a great city, palace towers,
Onion-shaped church domes, tall spires,
All walled about with gleaming white.
He wakes the Queen. 'Is this our fate?'
She cries, with joy. He says, 'I see:
My swan's been working busily.'
They walked forward, filled with wonder;
A gate opens; they're passing under
The walls, bells rang from every spire,
Crowds throng to meet them, a church choir
Praises God, gold coaches spill
Splendid lords and ladies; all
Exalt them, make obeisance
Exultantly before the Prince
And with a ducal cap he's crowned,
And hailed as lord of all the land;
With the Queen's blessing he put on,
That day, his new name: Duke Guidón.

The wind roams on the sea, and drives
A little ship along the waves;
Crowded together in their ship,
Under full sail, the sailors gape,
Seeing a wondrous miracle
On an island they know well:
A new city, crowned with gold,
Where barren mounds had been of old.
Cannons fire and bid them moor.
The merchants make fast to the pier;

The Duke receives them as his guests,
Gives them food and drink – the best.
'What, sailors, is your merchandise,
And where do you sail?' And one replies:
'We've sailed as far as we are able,
The world around; in fox and sable
We trade, and now we wish to rest,
Our term is up, we're sailing east,
Past the island of Buyán
Towards the land of King Saltán . . .'
The Duke spoke quietly to them then:
'I wish you God's speed, gentlemen,
Across the sea, against the sun,
Towards the famous King Saltan;
Tell him, I greet him courteously.'
The traders go, to cross the sea;
From the shore, good Duke Guidon
Watches them till they are gone.
Behold – atop the billows gliding
The white swan comes out of hiding.
'Hail, you fairest Prince of mine!
You wear a look of mist and rain.
Why's that? Has something saddened you?'
'Sadness-sorrow gnaws me through,
Sadness-sorrow harrows me:
My father I should like to see.'
Said swan to Prince: 'So that is why
You grieve! Well, would you like to fly
After the ship? Be, Prince, a gnat.' Her
Wings she beat, churned up the water,
Splashing him from head to foot.
Then he diminished to a dot,
Became a gnat, flew off and piped,
Caught up with the vessel, dropped

Very quietly down, to tuck
Himself quite nicely in a crack.

Towards the east, against the sun's
Rising, the merry vessel runs,
Past the island of Buyan,
To the realm of famed Saltan,
And the land they all desire
Is sighted already from afar.
They go ashore; King Saltan hastes
To bid the merchants be his guests,
And after them, to the palace, he
Flies, our brave lad, too small to see.
He sees: all in gold is shining
King Saltan, on his throne reclining,
Courtiers clustered round the throne
But somehow he looks sad, alone;
And the weaver and the cook,
With their mother, Babarook,
Sit the closest to him there,
They look him in the eyes, they stare.
The King invites his guests to sit,
And throws out questions while they eat:
'Where are you sailing for? How long,
My friends, have you been voyaging?
Are things foul abroad, or fair?
Seen any wonders anywhere?'
'We have sailed the whole world round,'
His guests reply. 'And we have found
It's not too bad; we can't complain.
And there's one wonder we have seen:
An island, craggy, harbourless
And dead, a godforsaken place;
A desert island; one young oak

Growing from the naked rock;
That's how it used to be. But now
A city has risen – God knows how –
With shining domes and gold-tipped spires,
Fertile gardens, palace towers.
Talk about castles in the air!
A Duke Guidon is ruler there.
He sends you greetings.' The great King
Slaps his knee, says, marvelling,
'How wonderful! I'm most impressed.
One day I'll take a trip due west
And visit there, as the Duke's guest.'
But the weaver and the cook,
With the crone, old Babarook,
Hate to think he might arrange
To visit somewhere rare and strange.
'That's a wonder, I don't think!'
Says the cook, with a sly wink
At the old crone and the weaver.
'A seaside city, well I never!
Listen, here's a real wonder:
A wood . . . a spruce-tree . . . sitting under
The spruce, a squirrel sings a song,
And nuts he nibbles, all day long,
But their little shells are gold,
Their kernels – pure emerald.
No seaside town comes up to that!'
King Saltan marvels; but the gnat
Is raging, raging – suddenly
He darts down at his aunt's right eye
And thrusts his tiny stinger in.
The cook cried, doubled up with pain.
Sister, crone, and maid with broom
Chase the gnat around the room,
Screaming, 'Wretch! We'll beat you flat!'

But through the window flies the gnat
And to his dukedom tranquilly
Makes his way across the sea.

   Again the Duke walks on the shore,
And gazes out, hour after hour;
Behold – atop the billows gliding
The white swan comes out of hiding.
'Hail, you fairest Prince of mine!
You wear a look of mist and rain.
Why's that? Has something saddened you?'
'Sadness-sorrow gnaws me through;
A wonder gleams before my eyes
And I must get it. Somewhere lies
A wood, and there's a squirrel under
A spruce, and – here's a real wonder –
Under the tree he sings a song,
And nuts he nibbles, all day long,
And their little shells are gold,
Their kernels – pure emerald;
But, it may be, people lie.'
Smiles the white swan in reply:
'No, what you've heard you may believe;
I know this marvel. Do not grieve,
My dear Prince; I'll be glad to grant,
For friendship's sake, the gift you want.'
The Duke went home, his soul much cheered;
Entering the wide courtyard –
What? Underneath a tall spruce-tree,
A squirrel sits, for all to see,
Gnaws a gold nut with his sharp teeth
Until an emerald glows beneath,
Gathers the shells into a pile,
And sings, whistling all the while,
For all good honest folk to hear:

'If in orchards nuts appear.'
The Duke stood, rooted there, amazed.
'Well, thanks,' he said. 'The Lord be praised,
And may He grant that lovely swan
Whatever joy her heart's set on.'
He made for the squirrel a crystal house;
Guards make sure no villains pass,
Clerks keep account of every gem;
To the Duke: wealth; the squirrel: fame.

The wind roams on the sea, and drives
A little ship along the waves;
Past the island, with full sail,
Past the hill-top capital:
Cannons fire and bid them moor.
The merchants make fast to the pier;
The Duke receives them as his guests,
Gives them food and drink – the best.
'What, sailors, is your merchandise,
And where do you sail?' And one replies:
'We've sailed the circle of the sun,
Trading in ponies from the Don,
We're tired, we'd like to rest in bed,
But a long trip still lies ahead –
Past the island of Buyan
Towards the land of King Saltan . . .'
The Duke spoke quietly to them then:
'I wish you God's speed, gentlemen,
Across the sea, against the sun,
Towards the famous King Saltan;
Tell him, I greet him courteously.'

The merchants bowed to their kind host,
Went out, and left that rocky coast.
The Duke stood watching from the shore

– And the swan's already cruising there.
The Duke begs: how his soul is yearning,
Tugging him, his heart is burning . . .
So again she instantly
Splashed him with her wing, and he
Changed to a fly, flew to the boat
Far out, and dropped, a tiny mote
In the blue heaven, a speck of black
– And tucked himself into a crack.

Towards the east, against the sun's
Rising, the merry vessel runs,
Past the island of Buyan,
To the realm of famed Saltan,
And the land they all desire
Is sighted already from afar.
They go ashore; King Saltan hastes
To bid the merchants be his guests,
And after them, to the palace, he
Flies, our brave lad, too small to see.
He sees: all in gold is shining
King Saltan, on his throne reclining,
Courtiers clustered round the throne
But somehow he looks sad, alone;
And the weaver, and the cook,
With the crone, old Babarook,
Sit the closest to him there,
With eyes like wicked toads, they stare.
The King invites his guests to sit,
And throws out questions while they eat:
'Where are you sailing for? How long,
My friends, have you been voyaging?
Are things foul abroad, or fair?
Seen any wonders anywhere?'
'We have sailed the whole world round,'

His guests reply. 'And we have found
It's not too bad; we can't complain.
And there's one wonder we have seen:
On the sea there lies an island,
A city on the rocky highland,
With shining domes and gold-tipped spires,
Fertile gardens, palace towers;
Before the palace grows a spruce,
Beneath it is a crystal house;
There a squirrel lives, quite tame,
But a little rascal all the same!
He whistles and sings a chirpy song,
And nuts he nibbles all day long,
All their little shells are gold,
Their kernels – pure emerald;
He has a guard, he has a servant,
They're most attentive and observant;
Keeping account of every nut
Is a state clerk; the troops salute
The marvellous squirrel, even the colonels!
Girls stow into chests the kernels,
And guineas cast from the gold shell
Are shipped worldwide. Everyone lives well,
Nice clothes, nice homes – the island thrives.
By the way, Duke Guidon gives
You his regards – he rules that land.'
Marvelling, slapping knee with hand,
King Saltan: 'Soon I'll take a trip,
Sail there in the royal ship,
Stay awhile with that kind Duke.'
But the weaver and the cook,
And the crone, old Babarook,
Hate to think he might arrange
To visit somewhere rare and strange.
Smiles the weaver: 'Well I never!

A squirrel who gnaws! That's really clever!
Nibbles nuggets, sweeps up gold,
Rakes up heaps of emeralds;
It happens a lot, it's nothing new,
Even if what you say is true.
But in the world there is a wonder:
The sea is boiling up like thunder,
The piling breakers crash and roar
Charging on a barren shore;
They swirl away, again come surging,
Then, from the ocean depths emerging,
Thirty-three heroes, handsome, dashing,
In armour, where the light keeps flashing,
Young giants, all alike; they cluster
On the seashore, as for a muster,
And with them is Uncle Chernomor.
Just picture it. I'll say no more.'
The merchants wisely hold their tongue,
To argue with her would be wrong.
Wonder is filling King Saltan,
But rage is filling Duke Guidon . . .
Rages and buzzes – and flies the fly
Directly at his aunt's left eye.
The weaver, as the fly flew in,
Cried 'Oi!' and doubled up with pain;
All cry: 'Catch it, catch it! Swat, swat!
Just you wait! We'll squash you flat!'
But he's already out to sea,
Flying home quite tranquilly.

　　Again the Duke walks by the blue
Ocean he's gazing at, or through;
Behold – atop the billows gliding
The white swan comes out of hiding.
'Hail, you fairest Prince of mine!

Still with a look of mist and rain
I see! Has something saddened you?'
'Sadness-sorrow gnaws me through;
There is a wonder – such a wonder! –
And I must see it. Surf like thunder
Charges on a barren shore,
Piling breakers crash and roar,
Swirl away, again come surging,
Then, from the oceans depths emerging,
Thirty-three heroes, handsome, dashing,
In armour, where the light keeps flashing,
Young giants, all alike; they cluster
On the seashore, as for a muster,
And with them is Uncle Chernomor.'
The swan replies: 'Prince, I am glad
It's nothing worse. Do not be sad,
These knights from the great deep I know:
They are my brothers. Quickly go,
And wait for them; be of good cheer,
For soon my brothers will appear.'

    The Duke went off, quite cheerfully,
And from his tower gazed at the sea;
Suddenly it roared like thunder,
The plashing billows burst asunder,
And leave on the pebbles thirty-three
Young knights; their armour flashingly
Reflects the sun; in pairs they go
Striding; his silver hair aglow
Also, strides Uncle, on his own,
And leads them to the city. Down
Leaps the Duke and runs to meet
The welcome strangers. In the street
There's running, people opening doors,

Shouting. Uncle Chernomor
To the good Duke: 'The swan's command
Has sent us to you, sweet Prince, and
We'll guard your city as she asks;
We each have our appointed tasks.
Every day we shall appear
Out of the waters, and march here
To guard your high walls; soon we'll talk,
But now the sea calls, we'll fall back;
To us, earth's air is burdensome.'
Therewith they turned and marched back home.

　　The wind roams on the sea, and drives
A little ship along the waves;
Past the island, with full sail,
Past the hill-top capital:
Cannons fire and bid them moor.
The merchants make fast to the pier.
The Duke receives them as his guests,
Gives them food and drink – the best;
'What, sailors, is your merchandise,
And where do you sail?' And one replies:
'We've sailed so far, our senses reel,
The whole world round, with Damask steel,
Pure silver, gold, and now like lead
We weigh, our last long voyage dread –
Past the island of Buyan
Towards the land of King Saltan . . .'
The Duke spoke quietly to them then:
'I wish you God's speed, gentlemen,
Across the sea, against the sun,
Towards the famous King Saltan.
Be sure to tell him that you bring
Duke Guidon's greetings to the King.'

The merchants bowed to their kind host,
Went out, and left that rocky coast.
The Duke stood watching from the shore
– The swan's already cruising there.
The Duke again: his soul is yearning,
He's being drawn, his heart is burning . . .
Splashed all over instantly
By her, he shrank, became a bee,
Flew off, with many a buzz and drone,
Overtook the merchantman,
Dropped instantly, as if to suck
A flower – and squeezed into a crack.

Towards the east, against the sun's
Rising, the merry vessel runs,
Past the island of Buyan,
To the realm of famed Saltan,
And the land they all desire
Is sighted already from afar.
They go ashore; King Saltan hastes
To bid the merchants be his guests,
And after them, to the palace, he
Goes, our brave lad, our bright bee,
And sees: all in gold is shining
King Saltan, on his throne reclining,
Courtiers clustered round the throne
But somehow he looks sad, alone;
And the weaver and the cook,
And the crone, old Babarook,
Sit the closest to him there –
Three women with four eyes to share.
The King invites his guests to sit,
And throws out questions while they eat:
'Where are you sailing for? How long,
My friends, have you been voyaging?

Are things foul abroad, or fair?
Seen any wonders anywhere?'
'We have sailed the whole world round,'
His guests reply. 'And we have found
It's not too bad; we can't complain.
And there's one wonder we have seen:
On the sea there lies an island,
A city on its rocky highland,
Every day there is a wonder:
The breakers pile like clouds to thunder,
Swirl away, again come surging,
Break asunder, and emerging
Come handsome heroes, thirty-three,
Light on their mail glints splendidly,
All alike, a giant cluster,
Formed into ranks, as for a muster,
By old Uncle Chernomor,
Who stands before them on the shore;
He leads them out in pairs to guard
That island. You would find it hard
To find a guard more valiant,
More trustworthy, more diligent.
A Duke Guidon's the ruler of
That lucky land. He sends his love.'
Marvelling at the tale they told,
King Saltan says: 'Before I'm old,
I'll see that Island of the Blessed;
Stay awhile as the Duke's guest.'
From the weaver and the cook
Not a word – but Babarook
Says with a crooked smile and wink:
'Why, that's a wonder, I don't think!
Knights coming out of the sea – that's hard
To swallow – ambling about on guard!
Whether it's truth or lies they tell us,

It's nothing very marvellous.
Much greater wonders can be found,
And here's a true story going round:
There's a princess who is so fair
You cannot take your eyes from her:
By day she dims God's radiant light,
And makes earth glitter in the night,
A moon gleams under her braided hair,
At her brow there glows a star.
Glides like a peacock; when she speaks
It's soft, as though the clear brook talks.
She's wonderful. I'll say no more.'
The wise merchants hold their tongue:
To argue with her would be wrong.
Wonder is filling King Saltan,
Rage is filling Duke Guidon,
Yet he feels sorry for the eyes
Of his old granny, and he flies,
Buzzing, at her nose instead:
The nose he stung was straightway red
And swollen, and her cry arose:
'Help, for God's sake! he's stung my nose!
Catch him! Swat him! Just you wait!
When I catch you . . .' It was too late;
Out through the window goes the bee,
Flew calmly home across the sea.

The Duke walks by the dark-blue sea
Again, and looks out constantly.
Behold – atop the billows gliding
The white swan comes out of hiding.
'Hail! you fairest Prince of mine!
Still with that look of mist and rain!
Why so? Has something saddened you?'
'Sadness-sorrow gnaws me through:

Other people marry: I
Look at girls, and walk right by.'
'Why, is there someone in your mind?'
'There is one girl I'd like to find:
She's a princess, and she's so fair
No one can take his eyes from her:
By day she dims God's radiant light,
And makes earth glitter in the night,
A moon gleams under her braided hair,
At her brow there glows a star.
Glides like a peacock; when she speaks
It's soft, as though the clear brook talks.
That's what they say – but is it true?'
He stopped, in fear. The white swan grew
Pensive awhile, and closed her eyes
A moment, in silence, then replies:
'Yes, it is true. But a wife's love
Is not to be thrown off like a glove
From your white hand, or tucked behind
Your belt. Think first, before you find
It is too late. Take thought. Think twice.
I serve you well with this advice.'
The Duke swore by his God above
That his heart yearned for married love,
His wish had not been born today,
He had thought long along the way;
It was high time: with all his soul
He'd walk, to find that beautiful
Princess, he'd walk, through nineteen lands,
To find her, and to win her hand.
At this the swan, with a deep sigh,
Said: 'Why go so far away?
Near is your fate, your destiny,
This princess, that you want – am I.'
Beating then her wings, she flew

High above the waves, and to
The shore dropped down, that pebbly shelf,
Ruffled her plumage, shook herself,
Became a girl with braided hair:
At her brow there glows a star,
It lights the earth; and when she speaks
It's soft, as though the clear brook talks.
The Duke embraces the princess,
Holds her to his white breast close,
And leads her swiftly to his mother.
They stand before her, close together,
Then the Duke's at her feet: 'My dear
Mama! Queen, dearest lady! Here
Before you is my chosen bride;
She'll be a daughter at your side,
We ask your blessing and consent
To your children's sacrament,
That we may live in peace and love.'
The mother weeps, and holds above
Their heads, bowed low, an ikon of
Our Lord and says: 'My children, God
Will bless you and He will reward.'
The Duke could not abide delay,
And quickly came the wedding-day;
Soon their marriage had begun;
Daughter they waited for, or son.

The wind roams on the sea, and drives
A little ship along the waves;
Past the isle, with bulging sail,
And the hill-top capital;
Cannons fire and bid them moor,
The merchants make fast to the pier.
The Duke receives them as his guests,
Gives them food and drink – the best;

'What, sailors, is your merchandise,
And where do you sail?' And one replies:
'We have sailed the whole world round,
With various wares, and now are bound
For home, due east; before us, all
That's left to make is a long haul
Past the island of Buyan
To the land of King Saltan.'
The Duke said to the merchants: 'Then
I wish you God's speed, gentlemen,
Across the sea, against the sun,
Towards the famous King Saltan;
You can remind your sovereign he
Promised to visit us, but we
Still haven't seen him. Give him our
Warmest regards.' They sail from shore;
The Duke however stayed at home,
Rather than leave his wife, this time.

    Towards the east, against the sun's
Rising, the merry vessel runs,
Past the island of Buyan,
To the realm of famed Saltan,
And the land they love so dearly
From afar-off is seen clearly;
They go ashore; King Saltan hastes
To bid the merchants be his guests.
The merchants see: upon his throne,
The King reclining, in his crown;
And the weaver and the cook,
With the crone, old Babarook,
Sit the closest to him there,
Three women with four eyes to share.
The King invites his guests to sit,
And throws out questions while they eat:

'Good to be home, is it? How long,
My friends, have you been voyaging?
Are things foul abroad, or fair?
Seen any wonders anywhere?'
'We have sailed the whole world round,'
His guests reply. 'And we have found
It's not too bad; we can't complain.
And there's one wonder we have seen:
On the sea there lies an island,
A city on its rocky highland,
With shining domes and gold-tipped spires,
Fertile gardens, palace towers;
Before the palace grows a spruce,
Beneath it is a crystal house;
There a squirrel lives, quite tame,
But a little rascal all the same!
He whistles and sings a chirpy song,
And nuts he nibbles all day long;
All the little shells are gold,
Their kernels – pure emerald;
The squirrel's taken care of, cherished.
But other wonders there have flourished:
The piling breakers crash and roar,
Surging up a barren shore,
Swirl away, again come surging,
Break asunder, and emerging
Come fine young heroes, thirty-three,
Light on their mail glints splendidly,
All alike, a giant cluster,
Formed into ranks, as for a muster,
By old Uncle Chernomor,
Who stands before them on the shore.
You'll never see a squad more valiant,
More trustworthy, more diligent.
Then there's the Duke's wife. She's so fair

No one can take his eyes from her.
By day she dims God's radiant light,
And makes earth glitter in the night.
A moon gleams under her braided hair,
At her brow there glows a star.
Duke Guidon rules that people. They
All sing his praises. By the way,
He sends regards, and his regret
You haven't made that visit yet
You've kept on promising. Why not go, King?
He seemed put out. He thinks you're joking.'

The King had heard enough – sent word
To his ships' captains: Be prepared.
But the weaver and the cook
And the crone, old Babarook,
Do not want him to arrange
To visit somewhere rare and strange.
But for once he cuts them short,
Stops their whining with a snort:
'Am I the King, or just a baby?
I'm sick of soon, one day, and maybe,
I'm going right now!' Stamped on the floor,
Swept from the room, and slammed the door.

By the window sits Guidon,
Gazing out. There's silence on
The sea, it does not rush, nor plash;
A barely barely trembling wash;
And over the hazy blue horizon
Into his view a fleet has risen:
On the spacious level ocean
Sails the fleet of King Saltan.
Duke Guidon cried out: 'Mama! Dear!
Dear Duchess! Papa's coming here.'

213

The fleet draws nearer. Duke Guidon
Aims a spyglass: standing on
The foredeck of his ship of state –
The King, his spyglass aiming straight
At him. The weaver and the cook
Stand with him, and old Babarook;
All, by their faces, are amazed
At this new country; dazzled, dazed.
Over the harbour, cannons boom,
Bells peal from every spire and dome.
The Duke's gone down, he's welcoming
His visitors ashore: the King,
Then the weaver and the cook,
And the crone, old Babarook;
Up to the city he led the King;
Tries to speak; can't say a thing.

The state apartments are all waiting;
At the gate gleams armour plating,
Clustered as for King's Inspection
Are fine lads, the realm's protection,
Thirty-three brave heroes, all
Alike, all handsome, dashing, tall,
Ready to fight and perish for
Their colonel, Uncle Chernomor.
The King has reached the courtyard; he
Sees, beneath a tall spruce-tree,
A squirrel; as it sings, it gnaws
A golden nut, then from it draws
The kernel out, an emerald stone;
The yard with golden shells is strewn.
The guests speed through, no time to ponder.
At last – what's this? Duchess? – A wonder!
A moon gleams under her braided hair,
At her brow there glows a star;

Glides forth like a peacock, brings
Mother-in-law with her. The King's
Thoughtful . . . staring . . . knows that face . . .
His heart leapt – now it starts to race!
Can it be? . . . How? . . . So many years . . .
He couldn't breathe . . . The King in tears
Embraces his Queen, and in his wide
Embrace, his young son, and the bride;
And all sit to a merry feast,
Talk, cries, hubbub, never ceased.
But the weaver and the cook,
And the crone, old Babarook,
Scattered, vanished, went to ground;
After a long search they were found.
Then they confessed to everything,
Started to cry and sob. The King,
Because of such rejoicing, just
Sent them home. Dizzily the day passed,
Hazily – King Saltan was led
Upstairs at length, half-drunk, to bed.
I was there; I had a drink,
Not many: beer and mead, I think.

[1831]

RUSALKA

The bank of the Dnieper. A mill.

MILLER *and his* DAUGHTER

MILLER:

Eh, you are all the same, you stupid girls.
If some gentleman of rank comes sniffing round
You ought to get hold of him pretty sharp.
How do you do that? By using your wits,
Giving a little here, denying a little there;
Hinting what you'd be like if you were married,
Because, of course, you intend to go spotless
To the altar. But if there's no hope of marriage –
Well, at least, get something for yourself
And for your family while you can. Remember
The old song: *He won't always love me,*
And bring me sweet perfumes . . . But, oh dear, no!
That's not your way, is it? You lose your head,
Fling yourself at him, do all he asks, for nothing!
You'd hang about his neck for a whole day,
And, before you know where you are, he's off,
And the scent is cold . . . You're left empty-handed.
Haven't I said to you a hundred times,
Take care, look after yourself, my girl,
Don't ruin your chances of prosperity
By letting the prince slip through your fingers;
Don't sell yourself cheap. But I might as well
Talk to the wind. It's no good sitting here
Crying your eyes out; that won't bring him back.

DAUGHTER:

What makes you think he's never coming back?
What makes you think I've lost him?

216

MILLER: It's all too clear,
    If you ask me. How many times a week
    Did he visit us, h'm? Every blessed day.
    And sometimes he'd come back for a second nibble.
    Then he started slacking off, and now
    It's nine days since he's been. You've lost him, girl.

DAUGHTER:
    He's busy; do you think he has no duties?
    He's not a miller, he can't stand around
    Letting the water work for him. He says
    There's no work in the world as hard as his.

MILLER:
    Oh, I dare say that's true! I bleed for him –
    Hunting the fox and hare, stuffing his belly,
    Browbeating servants, seducing stupid girls
    Like you. Poor fellow! Backbreaking work! But I
    Just take it easy! The water works for me!
    Well, let him take my place, and soil his hands –
    Everything leaking and rotting and needing repair.
    If only you had had the sense to ask him
    For a small sum, to put the mill to rights.

DAUGHTER:
    Ah!

MILLER:
        What is it?

DAUGHTER: Sh! I can hear hoofbeats . . .
    It's him, it's him!

MILLER: Remember my advice;
    Don't forget, girl . . .

217

DAUGHTER: He's come! You see, he's come!

[*Enter* PRINCE. *The groom leads away his horse.*]

PRINCE:
My dear! . . . Good day to you, miller.

MILLER: Gracious Prince,
You are most welcome. You've stayed away too long,
Too long. I'll go and prepare some food for you.

[*Exit.*]

DAUGHTER:
Ah, so you've remembered me at last!
Aren't you ashamed to have tormented me?
Every day I've waited, expecting you.
What wild and torturing thoughts came into my head!
And how I frightened myself! I saw you lying
At the foot of a cliff, or buried in a swamp,
Thrown by your horse; I thought a bear had killed you
When you were hunting; or that you were ill;
Even – that you'd stopped loving me . . . Thank God,
You're alive and well; and you still love me, don't you?
As much as ever?

PRINCE: As much as ever, dearest.
More than ever.

SHE: Yet you look sad; what's happened?

PRINCE:
Sad? No, of course not. – No, I'm full of joy,
Just to be seeing you. You make me happy.

SHE:

    No, when you're happy you come rushing towards me,
    And call out, 'Where's my pigeon?' when you're still
    A long way off. And then you kiss me and
    You ask me questions: Am I glad to see you?
    Did I expect you here so early? . . . But
    Today you listen to me and say nothing;
    You haven't hugged me, haven't kissed my eyes;
    Something is wrong, I know. What is it? Are
    You annoyed with me? I did something that upset you?

PRINCE:

    You've done nothing. I'm no good at pretence.
    You're right. My heart is very heavy – and
    You cannot lighten it with tenderness;
    Cannot dispel my grief, or even share it.

SHE:

    It would be dreadful to me if I could not
    Grieve with one grief, with you. So share it with me.
    If you allow it – I will cry; if not –
    I promise I won't vex you with one tear.

PRINCE:

    Why put it off? The sooner out, the better.
    My dear, there is no lasting happiness
    On earth – you know that; neither a high rank,
    Nor beauty, strength, nor riches, can protect us
    From evil fortune. You and I were happy,
    Weren't we? At least, I know that I was happy,
    Happy with you, in your love. Whatever is
    To come, I shan't forget you. What I lose –
    Nothing in the world can take its place.

SHE:

I do not understand what you are saying,
But I am frightened. There is some ill fate
Hanging over us, you're saying? Some deep sorrow;
A separation?

PRINCE: You've guessed. Separation.

SHE:

But what can part us? Can't I follow you,
On foot if need be, wherever you may go?
I'll dress up as a boy. I'll be your servant –
On the road, on the battlefield, anywhere –
I'm not afraid of war – if only I
Can see you. No, I don't believe it's true:
You're testing me, in some way; or you're joking.
Don't joke about such things!

PRINCE: It's not a joke.
I'm not in a joking mood, today. Nor am
I putting you to the test; I don't need to.
I'm not going on a journey, or to war.
I'll be at home. Yet we must part forever.

SHE:

Wait. I understand it, everything . . .
You're getting married.

[*The* PRINCE *is silent.*]

You're getting married!

PRINCE:

I must. There's no way out. Don't blame me for it.
Princes are not like girls, at liberty

To choose according to their hearts; the choice
Is made by others, for the sake of others . . .
God, and time, will comfort you. Please don't
Forget me; take this headband as a keepsake
– Here, I'll put it on. And I have brought
A necklace, too – please take it. One more thing:
I promised this to your father. Give it to him.

[*He hands her a bag of gold.*]

Goodbye.

SHE: Wait; I had something to tell you . . .
I have forgotten.

PRINCE: Think.

SHE: I would have done
Anything for you . . . That's not it . . . Wait –
It isn't possible you can be leaving me
Forever . . . That's not it either . . . Ah! I remember:
Today I felt your child move.

PRINCE: My poor girl!
What can be done? You must take care of yourself
If only for his sake; you needn't worry,
I'll see that you and your child are taken care of.
In time, perhaps, I'll even come myself
To pay you a visit. All will be well, don't cry.
Let me embrace you now, just one more time.

[*On his way out.*]

Ouf! It's over – that's a load off my mind.
I expected storms, but it went off fairly smoothly.

[*Exit. She remains motionless.*]

MILLER [*entering*]:

    Won't you come into the millhouse, sir? . . . Where is he?
    Where's the Prince gone? Oh yes, yes, yes! – let's *see*:
    Phew! what a headband! Glittering with gems!
    It blazes! oh, and pearls too! . . . Well, I say!
    This is a royal present. I take back
    All my complaints, girl. And what's that? A bag!
    Not money, is it? Why are you standing there
    Not saying a word, as if you were dumb? Have you
    Got lockjaw, girl, or have you lost your wits
    From such a windfall?

DAUGHTER: I loved him so much.
    It isn't possible. I don't believe it.
    Is he a wild beast? Is his heart shaggy?

MILLER:

    What are you talking about?

DAUGHTER: Oh father, tell me,
    What can I have done to anger him?
    Is all my beauty gone in one short week?
    Or maybe he's been made to drink some potion? . . .

MILLER:

    What's wrong?

DAUGHTER: He's gone, father; left me. Ridden away,
    And like a fool I let him go, I didn't
    Hang on to his cloak, or seize his reins
    And let myself be dragged along. I should
    Have made him hack my hands off at the wrists,
    Or trample me beneath the hooves!

MILLER: You're mad!

222

DAUGHTER:

    No, you don't see; princes aren't free to choose,
    As girls are, by their hearts . . . They're only free
    To promise, weep, implore, and say to you:
    I'll take you to a sunny, secret room
    In my palace, and array you in red velvet.
    They're free to teach you to fly out at midnight,
    Hearing their call, and stay with them till dawn
    Behind the mill. Their princely hearts are touched
    By our small woes – and then goodbye, all will
    Be well, don't cry; love who you wish.

MILLER:

    I see – so that's it.

DAUGHTER: But who's taken him?
    I shall find out. And I shall tell that creature:
    Keep your claws off the Prince; for two she-wolves
    Can't hunt in the same gully.

MILLER: Foolish slut!
    If the Prince wants to find himself a bride,
    Who can stop him? That's the way things go.
    Haven't I told you . . .

DAUGHTER: It was all right, you think,
    For him to take his leave, so pleasantly,
    With gifts – with money! Buying himself off,
    Silvering my tongue to keep it silent, so
    No word of this should reach his pure young wife.
    Ah yes, I had forgotten – this money-bag
    Is yours for being so kind to him, allowing
    Your daughter to trail after him, not keeping
    Too strict an eye on her . . . He's paid you well
    For my ruin.

[*Gives him the bag.*]

MILLER:　　　　What punishment has God reserved
For my old age! What have I lived to hear!
What cruel words you speak, to your own father.
You are my only child, the only comfort
I have in the whole world, and I am old.
I couldn't help but spoil you a little,
Could I? The Lord has punished me for not
Being firmer with you.

DAUGHTER:　　　　　　Oh, how warm it is . . .
I'm stifling. A cold snake's wound about my neck . . .
A snake – he's looped a snake around my throat,
Not pearls.

[*She tears the pearls off.*]

MILLER:　　Think what you're doing.

DAUGHTER:　　　　　　　　And so I'd tear
That wicked woman who . . .

MILLER:　　　　　　　You're raving, child,
You're raving.

DAUGHTER [*taking off the headband*]:
　　　　　　There's my crown, my crown of shame!
The bridal crown the Devil put on my head
The moment when I turned away from all
I once held dear. – So, vanish then, my crown!

[*She throws the headband into the Dnieper.*]

Now everything is over.

[*She throws herself into the river.*]

THE OLD MAN [*falling*]:   O grief, O grief!

The Prince's palace.

A wedding. The bridal pair sit at table.
GUESTS. CHOIR OF YOUNG GIRLS.

MATCHMAKER:
We've made a merry, joyful wedding, truly.
And now, good health to you, Prince, and to your
Sweet young Princess! God give you both long life,
In love and harmony. And God grant us –
To celebrate often with you at your table!
Our songstresses, why have you fallen silent?
White swans, have you no more to sing to us?
I can't believe you've sung us all your songs?
Or have your throats dried up from so much singing?

CHOIR: Matchmaker, matchmaker,
                    Stupid old matchmaker!
                    Went to fetch the bride,
                    Took a stroll outside,
                    Round the back, you know,
                    For she'd drunk too much,
                    A keg of ale or so,
                    Soaked the cabbage-patch,
                    On the fence she stumbled,
                    To the gatepost mumbled:
                    Gentle gate, I pray,
                    Point me out the way
                    To the bride's abode.
                    Matchmaker, it says,

225

You must guess the road,
I can't help, unless
A kopeck you can spare:
For I can't live on air,
No more than can the choir
Of gentle maids you hire.

MATCHMAKER:

You rascals, what a song to choose! You shouldn't
Tease an old woman! Oh well, here, take this.

[*Gives the* GIRLS *money.*]

A SINGLE VOICE:

Over the pebbles and over the yellow sand
Runs the swift river, and two little fishes
Swim in that swift river – little roaches.
O my roach-sister, have you heard the news,
How yesterday a girl drowned in our river,
And how she cursed her lover as she drowned?

MATCHMAKER:

O girls! Why do you sing such a sad song?
It's not a song fit for a wedding; no.
Who chose it, h'm?

THE GIRLS: Not I – not I – it wasn't us . . .

MATCHMAKER:

Who sang it then?

[*Whispering and confusion among the* GIRLS.]

PRINCE: I know who sang it to us.

[*He leaves the table and speaks quietly to the* GROOM.]

She's found her way here. Get her away at once.

And then find out who let her in.

[*The* GROOM *searches among the* GIRLS.]

PRINCE [*sitting down, to himself*]:   If she's
Intent on stirring up trouble, there's no end
To the shame and mischief she could cause me.

GROOM:
Sir, I can't find her.

PRINCE: Look again. She's here,
I know. She sang that song.

A GUEST: What splendid mead!
It goes straight to the head – and to the legs!
A trifle bitter: sweeten it for us.

[*The* BRIDE *and* GROOM *kiss. A faint cry is heard.*]

PRINCE:
That's her! Her jealous cry.
          [*To the* GROOM.] Well?

GROOM:

                                        She's not here.

PRINCE: Fool.

BEST MAN [*rising*]:   Isn't it time we let the happy couple
Retire, while at the door we shower them
With hops?

[*All rise.*]

MATCHMAKER:
                         High time. Come, serve the cockerel.

227

[*The* BRIDE *and* GROOM *are served with roast cockerel, then
showered with hops and led to their bedroom.*]

MATCHMAKER:
> Princess, my dear, don't cry, don't be afraid,
> Do as he wants.

[*The* BRIDE *and* GROOM *retire to their bedroom, the guests all take
their leave, except for the* MATCHMAKER *and the* BEST MAN.]

BEST MAN:　　　　　Where is my glass? All night
> I have to ride around beneath their windows;
> A glass to strengthen me won't come amiss.

MATCHMAKER [*pouring him a glass*]
> Here's to our health.

BEST MAN:　　　　　Ouf! Thank you. It
> Went off quite well, I think, don't you? The feast
> Was splendid.

MATCHMAKER:　Yes, thank God, all went off well. –
> Except for one thing.

BEST MAN:　　　　　Why, what was that?

MATCHMAKER:　　　　　　　　The song
> They sang. It wasn't a wedding-song, but God
> Knows what it was.

BEST MAN:　　　　Oh well, they're only girls.
> But yes, of course, it was a tasteless joke –
> And at a royal wedding too. A shame.
> But – I must to my horse. It's going to seem

A longer night for me than for the Prince.
Goodnight, old mother.

[*Exit.*]

MATCHMAKER: Ah, my heart's not easy.
This marriage was not made in a good hour.

A room in the palace.

The PRINCESS *and her* NURSE

PRINCESS:
Hark – do I hear horns? No, he's not come.
Ah, dear nanny, when he was courting me
He never left my side, he could not keep
His eyes from me. He married me, and now
Everything's different. He wakens me at dawn
With shouts to servants that his horse be saddled;
Then rides out, God knows where, till night; and when
He's back, he scarcely has a tender word
For me, can hardly bear for me to touch him.

NURSE:
It's nothing new, poor child; a husband is
A cock – kiri-ku-ku! He flaps his wings
And off. A woman's like a broody hen,
Guarding the nest and hatching out her chicks.
Before he's got you, he will sit with you
From morn till night, won't eat, won't drink, just gazing
Into your eyes. But once he's married – there's
So much he has to do: must visit neighbours,
Or go off hawking with his falcons; then
He's off to war. Now here, now there – but never

229

At home in peace.

PRINCESS: Do you think he has some girl
He goes to see?

NURSE: Don't speak of such a thing.
Where would he find a girl who equals you?
You're beautiful, intelligent, and gentle.
Why should he look for someone else? Don't even
Think such a wicked thought, my child.

PRINCESS: If only
My prayers were answered and we had a baby!
Then I would win his love afresh . . . They're back!
The courtyard's full of huntsmen. Yet I can't
Pick out my husband.

[*Enter a* HUNTSMAN.]

HUNTSMAN: The Prince commanded us
To ride for home.

PRINCESS: But where is he?

HUNTSMAN: He's stayed
Alone in the forest on the Dnieper's bank.

PRINCESS:
You left him there alone! Oh, what fine servants!
What loyal, diligent servants! Back again,
At once – go, at the gallop! Find him, tell him
It was I who sent you. [*Exit the* HUNTSMAN.]
                                        Ah, my God, the forests
Are full of beasts, by night, and savage men,
And wicked spirits wander – light the candle

Before the ikon, quickly.

NURSE: At once, my light,
At once . . .

The Dnieper. Night.

RUSALKAS: In a cheerful swarm
                 We swim up at night
                 From the depths to warm
                 Ourselves in the moon's light.
                 It's pleasant to leave
                 Our murky home,
                 It's pleasant to cleave
                 The river's glass dome,
             To hear our teasing voices fly
             Through the hollows of the air,
             Carried on the winds that dry
             Speedily our wet green hair.

ONE: Quiet, quiet! something stirred,
                 Rustled in the undergrowth.

ANOTHER: Between the moon and us I heard
                 Someone walking on the earth.

                 [*They hide.*]

PRINCE:
    Sad and familiar spot! I recognize
    These landmarks – there's the mill! A ruin now;
    The cheerful racket of its wheels is silent;
    The millstone sleeps – the old man must be dead.
    He didn't grieve for his poor daughter long.

231

This was a path, I'm sure – it's overgrown,
No one has come this way for many a year;
There was a little garden here, fenced round –
Could it have grown into this tangled copse?
Ah, there's the sacred oak, where she and I
Embraced; she let her head droop, and fell silent . . .
Is it possible? . . .

[*He goes up to the tree, a shower of leaves falls on him.*]

What can this mean? The leaves
Withered before my eyes, curled up and fell
On me, like a faint rustling fall of ashes.
The tree is black and naked, it's accursed.

[*An* OLD MAN *enters, ragged, half-naked.*]

OLD MAN:
Good day, son-in-law.

PRINCE: Who are you?

OLD MAN: I'm
The raven of this place.

PRINCE: Is it possible? –
The miller.

OLD MAN: Hardly the miller any more!
I sold the mill to spirits behind the stove,
And gave the money to the water-nymphs
To keep it safe; it's in my daughter's keeping.
They've buried the money in the Dnieper's sand.
A one-eyed fish keeps guard on it.

PRINCE: Poor man,
He's mad. His thoughts are scattered like the clouds
After a storm.

OLD MAN: Why didn't you come last night?
We had a splendid feast, we waited for you.

PRINCE:
Who waited for me?

OLD MAN: Who? My daughter, of course.
You know, I look at everything through my fingers,
I don't mind what you do, she can sit up
All night with you, till cockcrow. Mum's the word.

PRINCE:
Unhappy miller.

OLD MAN: I've told you, I'm a raven,
Not a miller. It was a strange thing: when she threw
Herself in the river (do you remember?) I
Ran after her and wanted to fling myself
From that rock there, only – just then – I felt
Two strong wings lift me underneath the armpits
And I was carried into the air. Since then
I have been flying about; sometimes I'll peck
At a dead cow, and sometimes perch on a grave,
And caw.

PRINCE: And who looks after you, poor man?

OLD MAN:
Ah yes – well, that's no easy thing, you know.
I'm old and mischievous. But, thank God, I'm
Well taken care of by the water-baby.

PRINCE:
    Who?

OLD MAN:
      My grandchild.

PRINCE:
                 He's beyond understanding.
Old man, you'll die of hunger in these woods,
Or some beast will attack you. Wouldn't you like
To come and live with me?

OLD MAN:
              Live in your palace!
No, thank you very much! You'd lure me in,
And then, most likely, strangle me with pearls.
Here I'm alive, and fed, and free. No, no,
I won't go with you.

               [*Exit.*]

PRINCE:
            All this is my doing!
It's terrible, to go mad. I'd rather die.
We look upon a dead man with respect.
We pray for him. And death makes all men equal.
But a man who's lost his reason is no longer
A man. Gifted with speech in vain, he cannot
Control his words, he calls a beast his brother,
And is derided by his fellow men.
Everyone can make free with him, and God
Himself can't judge him. O that poor old man!
The sight of him has opened up the wound,
The torments of remorse.

HUNTSMAN: At last! He's here!
   Are you all right? We thought we'd never find you.

PRINCE:
   Why have you come back?

HUNTSMAN: The Princess sent us.
   She was afraid for you.

PRINCE: Her care's unwelcome.
   Am I a child, who must walk with his nanny?

   [*Exit. The* RUSALKAS *rise up from the river.*]

RUSALKA:
         Sisters, shall we hurry after,
         Turn their gallop into flight,
         And with splashes, whistling, laughter,
         Drive their horses mad with fright?

         It's too late. The forest darkens,
         And the deeps grow colder yet,
         Now the village stirs and hearkens
         For the cock. The moon has set.

ONE: Can't we wait a moment, sister?

ANOTHER:
         No, it's time; we cannot wait.

         There – the crowing. Our Tsaritsa
         Doesn't like us to be late.

              [*They vanish.*]

At the bottom of the Dnieper.
Palace of the Rusalkas.

The RUSALKAS *sit spinning around their* TSARITSA.

RUSALKA-QUEEN:
　　Sisters, leave your spinning. The sun has set.
　　Enough. A shaft of moonlight gleams above us.
　　Swim up and play a while, beneath the sky,
　　But make sure you don't bother anyone
　　Tonight, don't tickle passers-by, or clog
　　The fishermen's nets with weed and mud, nor lure
　　The child into the water with tales of fishes.

　　　　　　　　[*Enter the* WATER-BABY.]

　　Where have you been?

DAUGHTER:　　　　　　　　I've been out on the land
　　To visit grandfather. He keeps begging me
　　To gather up the money that he threw
　　Down to the river-bed for us, long ago,
　　And bring it to him. I've looked and looked.
　　I think I know what money looks like, but
　　I'm not sure. Anyway, I brought him out
　　A handful of bright shells, all different colours,
　　And he was very pleased.

RUSALKA:　　　　　　　　The crazy miser!
　　Now listen, darling. I am going to trust you
　　With something important. Tonight a man will come
　　Down to our river-bank. Watch out for him
　　And go to meet him. That man is close to us,
　　He is your father.

236

DAUGHTER: The same one who left you,
  To marry a woman?

RUSALKA: The very same; greet him
  Tenderly, dear, and tell him all you've learned
  From me about your birth; tell him about me.
  And if he asks if I've forgotten him
  Or not, tell him I still remember him
  And love him, and long to see him. Do
  You understand?

DAUGHTER: I understand.

RUSALKA: Then go.

          [*Alone.*]

  Ever since the time when, out of my mind,
  A desperate and rejected girl, I threw
  Myself into the Dnieper, and awoke,
  Deep down, as a cold and powerful rusalka,
  I've brooded every day on my revenge,
  And now, at last, it seems my hour has come.

The bank.

PRINCE:
  Unwillingly I come to these sad shores,
  Drawn by some unknown power. Everything here
  Reminds me of the past, and tells the story
  – Dear to me, though it is melancholy –
  Of my bright, carefree youth. Here, long ago,
  Love ran to meet me: free, spontaneous love;
  And I was happy . . . crazy! to have turned
  My face away from that happiness. Such mournful,

237

Mournful thoughts, deeper than tears. That meeting,
Yesterday, has brought them flooding back.
That poor madman! How terrible he is!
Maybe today again I'll meet her father,
And he'll agree to leave the woods and come
To live with us . . .

[*The water-baby emerges on the bank.*]

What's this I see?
My pretty little child, where have you come from?

[1832]

THE TALE OF THE GOLDEN COCKEREL

SOMEWHERE, and some time ago
(That's as much as scholars know),
Lived the glorious Tsar Dadón.
Fierce was he from his youth on,
To his neighbours gave offence
With bold acts of violence;
But, when age encumbered him,
Tsar Dadon began to dream
Quiet ending to his labours:
Just when his long-suffering neighbours
Gained the courage to hit back,
Mounted many a fierce attack.
Keeping their wild hordes at bay
Meant he had to feed and pay
Numerous armies, a great host
Stretched around the frontier-posts.
Even so, they were outnumbered;
Though his generals never slumbered,
On the southern front arrayed,
They would hear about the raid
Being mounted from the east;
And the panic never ceased:
When the eastern breach was sealed,
There was no defensive shield
Held in readiness to halt
Fleets that moved in to assault
Seaboard cities. The Tsar wept,
Many a night he never slept.
What a life, for an old man!
So the wretched Tsar Dadon
Summoned to his court a seer—
A eunuch, and astrologer.

When he came, he gave the old
Emperor a cock of gold.
'Put this bird,' he told the Tsar,
'On your country's highest spire;
My gold cockerel will be
Your true watchman: quietly
He will sit if all is quiet
In your realm, but should a riot
Spring up somewhere, or a great
Army seem to pose a threat
To your borders, or some band
Cross by stealth into your land,
Anything to cause alarm,
Instantly he'll raise his comb,
Ruffle up his feathers, crow,
Swing around to let you know
Where the danger lies.' The King
Thanked the eunuch, promising
Golden mountains. 'If it's true,'
Says the joyful monarch, 'You
Will be recompensed. We can't
Thank you enough. And we will grant
Your first wish as though it were
Our very own.'

From a high spire
Gazed the golden cockerel. When
Danger anywhere was seen,
Instantly he gave the warning,
Like the first cock of the morning –
Turned towards the danger, crew
Lustily, 'Kiri-ku-ku,
You be careful on your throne!'
And the neighbours settled down,
Dared not carry on the war,

For the Tsar was there before
They could muster their attack;
Savagely he drove them back.

    One year passes peacefully,
Then another; tranquilly
Sits the cockerel on the spire.
Then one day the drowsing Tsar
Was awakened by a shout,
Heard his officers cry out:
'Father of the people! Master!
Sovereign, awake! Disaster!'
'What's the matter, gentlemen?'
Yawning, mumbles Tsar Dadon.
'Eh? . . . Who's there? . . .' 'The golden cock
Crows again, and all your flock
Trembles,' cries the general;
'Panic's seized the capital.'
To his window goes the Tsar,
Sees the cockerel on the spire
Wildly fluttering; he's veered east.
'Soldiers, to your mounts! Make haste!
Hurry!' says the monarch, and
Due east under the command
Of his eldest son they ride.
Terror and confusion died
Into silence, as the gold
Cock stopped crowing, and the old
Tsar dozed again.

                    Eight days go by.
Have they met the enemy?
There's no news, no message for
Dadon. The cock crows once more,
Urgently, and Tsar Dadon

Straightway bids his younger son
Set out eastwards, with another
Army, to assist his brother;
Once again the cockerel
Grows calm . . . Eight days pass by; still
Nothing is heard, no news! The people
Live in dread; upon the steeple
Crows again the golden weather-
Vane; the monarch calls together
Yet a third host, leads it east,
Thinking he must try, at least,
To discover what's gone wrong.

Day and night they march along,
Till the soldiers' spirits fail,
Find the trek unbearable;
On and on; the Tsar's not found
Battle-site or burial mound
Or abandoned camp. He thinks:
'What's this wonder?' The sun sinks
On the eighth day; now the plain
Yields to mountainous terrain;
Still the troops plod onwards, and
There, with frozen peaks all round,
They can see a tent of silk;
And the mountains white as milk
Fold about it a serene
Wondrous quietness; between
Gloomy walls of a ravine
Lies the beaten army. Tsar
Dadon strides to the tent . . . And there –
Dreadful sight! his eyes grow dim:
His two sons in front of him,
Like a nightmare, lying dead,
Unarmoured and unhelmeted;

Each has driven his sword home
In the other. Their steeds roam
In the meadow, over trodden
Grass, over the blood-sodden
Sward . . . The Tsar wailed: 'O, my sons!
Both my falcons fallen at once
Into snares! Unbearable!
Death, come soon for me.' Then all
After Dadon wailed and moaned,
Thunder through the valley groaned
And the mountains' heart was rent.
Suddenly the silken tent
Was flung open . . . And Dadon
Thought he saw the shining dawn,
But the Queen of Shemakhá
Quietly stood before the Tsar.
Like a bird, who sings at night,
Struck dumb by the sun's first light,
He stood rooted to the spot,
Looked her in the eyes, forgot,
In her presence, his two sons.
Smiling, the maid took Dadon's
Hand, and courteously she led him
To her tent, and there she fed him
Every kind of food and laid him
On a bed of rich brocade
To rest. For just a week he stayed
Feasting with her; and the King,
Charmed, enraptured, let her bring
Meat, wine, minstrels – everything.

　　Finally the Tsar strikes camp,
Sets off home. Behind him tramp
His armed force, and at his side
Sits the maiden. Rumour rides

Swiftly ahead, and spreads about
Truths and falsehoods. Crowds spill out
To the city gates and meet
The returning host; they greet
Their brave soldiers with huzzas,
Turn and run after the Tsar's
Chariot . . . As he rode along,
Smiling, waving – in the throng
Milling round them he caught sight
Of someone he knew . . . a white
Saracen hat and hair that shone
White as feathers of a swan,
Lank hair, straggling to his tunic . . .
There was his old friend, the eunuch.
'Greetings, father,' said the Tsar;
'Tell me, what is your desire?
Step up closer, I can't hear.'
'Majesty!' replied the seer –
'Let us settle our account.
You have promised you would grant
My first wish, as you recall.
Well then, I should like that girl.
Yes, the Queen of Shemakha.
That's all. Give me her.' The Tsar
Stared at the astrologer
Disbelieving, his face red.
'What? What did I hear?' he said.
'Either the devil's got in you,
Or you've lost your mind. It's true
I did promise a reward,
But your wish is quite absurd.
What would you want a maiden for?
Enough! Do you know who we are?
Ask of me my finest mare
From the royal stables, or

I will make you a boyar;
Ask of me my treasury,
Or take half my kingdom.' 'I
Don't want anything, you see,'
Said the wise man to the Tsar.
'Just the Queen of Shemakha.'
'Devil take you!' the King spat.
'You'll get nothing, then! That's that!
You have brought it on yourself,
You old sinner. Now, clear off!
Thank your stars your skin's still whole.
Drag away the old numskull!'
But the staunch old man resisted;
Argued with the King; insisted –
Something you don't lightly do
With a king, or people who
Think like kings: and Tsar Dadon
Raised his sceptre, crashed it down:
Fell, the old man; fled, his soul;
Shuddered, all the capital; –
But the Queen of Shemakha:
'Hee-hee-hee!' and 'Ha-ha-ha!'
Nothing frightened her. The Tsar
Smiled at her and took her arm
Tenderly, hid his alarm.
Rides now into town . . . There is
Suddenly a ringing noise
Overhead, and everyone
Saw the cockerel flutter down
From his steeple, aiming straight
For the chariot, and it sat
On the Tsar's head; comb erect,
Feathers ruffled, the bird pecked
At the Tsar's pate, and was gone,
Soaring up . . . And King Dadon

Tumbled from the chariot, –
Groaned once – and lay lifeless. But
No one sees the lovely queen:
Gone, as if she had not been.
This tale's false, but useful for
Lads inclined to be cocksure.

[1833]

THE BRONZE HORSEMAN

A Tale of St Petersburg

Introduction

On a shore washed by desolate waves, *he* stood,
Full of high thoughts, and gazed into the distance.
The broad river rushed before him; a wretched skiff
Sped on it in solitude. Here and there,
Like black specks on the mossy, marshy banks,
Were huts, the shelter of the hapless Finn;
And forest, never visited by rays
Of the mist-shrouded sun, rustled all round.

And he thought: From here we will outface the Swede;
To spite our haughty neighbour I shall found
A city here. By nature we are fated
To cut a window through to Europe,
To stand with a firm foothold on the sea.
Ships of every flag, on waves unknown
To them, will come to visit us, and we
Shall revel in the open sea.

A hundred years have passed, and the young city,
The grace and wonder of the northern lands,
Out of the gloom of forests and the mud
Of marshes splendidly has risen; where once
The Finnish fisherman, the sad stepson
Of nature, standing alone on the low banks,
Cast into unknown waters his worn net,
Now huge harmonious palaces and towers
Crowd on the bustling banks; ships in their throngs
Speed from all ends of the earth to the rich quays;

The Neva is clad in granite; bridges hang
Poised over her waters; her islands are covered
With dark-green gardens, and before the younger
Capital, ancient Moscow has grown pale,
Like a widow in purple before a new empress.

I love you, Peter's creation, I love your stern
Harmonious look, the Neva's majestic flow,
Her granite banks, the iron tracery
Of your railings, the transparent twilight and
The moonless glitter of your pensive nights,
When in my room I write or read without
A lamp, and slumbering masses of deserted
Streets shine clearly, and the Admiralty spire
Is luminous, and, without letting in
The dark of night to golden skies, one dawn
Hastens to relieve another, granting
A mere half-hour to night. I love
The motionless air and frost of your harsh winter,
The sledges coursing along the solid Neva,
Girls' faces brighter than roses, and the sparkle
And noise and sound of voices at the balls,
And, at the hour of the bachelor's feast, the hiss
Of foaming goblets and the pale-blue flame
Of punch. I love the warlike energy
Of Mars' Field, the uniform beauty of the troops
Of infantry and of the horses, tattered
Remnants of those victorious banners in array
Harmoniously swaying, the gleam of those
Bronze helmets, shot through in battle. O martial
Capital, I love the smoke and thunder
Of your fortress, when the empress of the north
Presents a son to the royal house, or when
Russia celebrates another victory
Over the foe, or when the Neva, breaking

Her blue ice, bears it to the seas, exulting,
Scenting spring days.

                    Flaunt your beauty, Peter's
City, and stand unshakeable like Russia,
So that even the conquered elements may make
Their peace with you; let the Finnish waves
Forget their enmity and ancient bondage,
And let them not disturb with empty spite
Peter's eternal sleep!

   There was a dreadful time – the memory of it
Is still fresh . . . I will begin my narrative
Of it for you, my friends. My tale will be sad.

1

November over darkened Petrograd.
With a roar of waves splashing against the edges
Of her shapely bounds, the Neva tossed
Like a sick man in his restless bed.
It was already late and dark; against
The window angrily the rain was beating,
And the wind blew, howling sadly. At that time
Came young Yevgeni home, from friends . . . We'll call
Our hero by this name. It's pleasant, and
Has long been congenial to my pen.
We do not need his surname, though perhaps
In times gone by it shone, under the pen
Of Karamzin, rang forth in our native legends;
But now it is forgotten by the world
And fame. Our hero lives in Kolomna, works
Somewhere, avoids the paths of the famous, mourns
Neither dead relatives nor the forgotten past.

And so, having come home, Yevgeni tossed
His cloak aside, undressed, lay down. But for
A long time could not fall asleep, disturbed
By divers thoughts. What did he think about?
About the fact that he was poor, by toil
Would have to earn honour and independence;
That God might have granted him more brains and money,
That there are lazy devils, after all,
For whom life is so easy! That he had been
A clerk for two years; he also thought the weather
Was not becoming any calmer; that
The river was still rising; as like as not,
The bridges on the Neva had been raised,
And for two or three days he would be cut off
From Parasha. At that point Yevgeni sighed
From his heart, and fell to dreaming like a poet.

'Get married? Me? Why not! It would be hard,
Of course; but then, I'm young and healthy, ready
To toil day and night; somehow or other
I'll fix myself a humble, simple shelter
Where Parasha and I can live in quiet.
After a year or two I'll get a job,
And Parasha will bring up our children . . . Then
We shall begin to live, and thus we'll go
Hand in hand to the grave, and our grandchildren
Will bury us . . .'

Thus he dreamed. And he felt sad that night,
And wished the wind would not howl gloomily,
The rain not beat so angrily at the window . . .

At last he closed his sleepy eyes. And now
The foul night thins, and the pale day draws on . . .
The dreadful day!

All night the Neva rushed
Towards the sea against the storm, unable
To overcome the madness of the winds . . .
She could no longer carry on the struggle . . .
By morning, throngs of people on her banks
Admired the spray, the mountains and the foam
Of maddened waters. But harried by the gale
Out of the gulf, the Neva turned back, angry,
Turbulent, and swamped the islands. The weather
Raged more fiercely, Neva swelled up and roared,
Bubbling like a cauldron; suddenly
Hurled herself on the city like a beast.
Everything ran before her, everything
Suddenly became deserted – suddenly
The waters flowed into the cellars underground,
The canals surged up to the railings,
And Petropolis floated up, like Triton,
Plunged to the waist in water.

Siege! Assault! The sly waves climb like thieves
Through the windows. Scudding boats smash the panes
With their sterns. Hawkers' trays, fragments of huts,
Beams, roofs, the wares of thrifty trading,
The chattels of pale poverty, bridges swept
Away by the storm, coffins from the buried
Cemetery – all float along the streets!

The people gaze upon the wrath of God
And await their doom. Alas! All's swept away:
Shelter and food – where shall they find them?

In that dread year the late Tsar in his glory
Still ruled Russia. He came out on to the balcony,
Sad, troubled, and said: 'Tsars cannot master
The divine elements.' He sat down and with thoughtful
Sorrowful eyes gazed on the dire disaster:

The squares like lakes; broad rivers of streets
Pouring into them. The palace a sad island.
The Tsar spoke – from end to end of the city,
Along streets near and far, a dangerous journey
Through the storm waters, generals set off
To save the people, drowning in their homes.

There, in Peter's square, where in the corner
A new house towers, where over the lofty porch
Two guardian lions stand like living creatures
With upraised paw – there sat, astride the marble
Beast, hatless, his arms crossed tightly,
Motionless and fearfully pale, Yevgeni.
He was afraid, poor fellow, not for himself.
He did not hear the greedy billow rise,
Lapping his soles; he did not feel the rain
Lashing his face, nor the wind, wildly howling,
Tear his hat from his head. His desperate gaze
Was fixed on one distant point. Like mountains,
There the waves rose up from the seething depths,
And raged, there the storm howled, there wreckage
Rushed to and fro . . . God, God! There –
Alas! – so close to the waves, almost by the gulf
Itself, is an unpainted fence and a willow
And a small ramshackle house: there they live,
A widow and her daughter, Parasha, his dream . . .
Or is all this a dream? Is all our life
Nothing but an empty dream, heaven's jest?

And he, as though bewitched, as if riveted
To the marble, cannot get down! Around him
Is water and nothing else! And, his back turned
To him, in unshakeable eminence, over
The angry river, the turbulent Neva, stands
The Image, with outstretched arm, on his bronze horse.

But now, satiated with destruction, wearied
By her insolent violence, the Neva drew back,
Revelling in the chaos she had caused,
And carelessly abandoning her booty.
Thus a marauder, bursting into a village with
His savage band, smashes, slashes, shatters,
And robs; shrieks, gnashing of teeth, violence,
Oaths, panic, howls! And weighed down by their plunder,
Fearing pursuit, exhausted, the robbers leave
For home, dropping their plunder on the way.

The water fell, the roadway was visible,
And my Yevgeni, in hope and fear and grief,
Hastened with sinking heart to the scarcely abated
River. But full of their victory the waves
Still seethed angrily, as though beneath them
Fires were smouldering; foam still covered them,
And heavily the Neva breathed, like a horse
Galloping home from battle. Yevgeni looks:
He sees a boat; he runs towards his find;
Shouts to the ferryman – and for ten kopecks
The carefree ferryman rows him across the billows.

And long the experienced oarsman struggled with
The stormy waves, and all the time the skiff
Was on the point of plunging with its rash crew
To the depths, between the ranges of the waves
– And at last he reached the bank.

                          The wretched man
Runs down a familiar street to familiar places.
He gazes, and can recognize nothing.
A dreadful vision! All is piled up before him:
This has been hurled down, that has been torn away;

The little houses have become twisted, others
Have completely collapsed, others have been shifted
By the waves; all around, as on a battlefield,
Corpses are strewn. Yevgeni rushes headlong,
Remembering nothing, exhausted by torments,
To the place where fate awaits him with unknown tidings,
As with a sealed letter. And now he is
Already rushing through the suburb, and here
Is the bay, and close by is the house . . .
What is this? . . .

                He stopped. Went back and turned.
Looked . . . walked forward . . . looked again.
Here is the place where their house stood;
Here is the willow. There were gates here – swept
Away, evidently. But where is the house?
And, full of gloomy anxiety, he walks, he walks
Around, talks loudly to himself – and then,
Striking his forehead with his hand, he laughed.

  Darkness fell upon the city, shaking
With terror; long its people did not sleep,
But talked among themselves of the past day.

  Dawn's light shone over the pale capital
And found no trace of the disaster; loss
Was covered by a purple cloak. And life
Resumed its customary order. People
Walked coldly, impassively, along cleared streets.
Government officials, leaving their night's shelter,
Went to their jobs. The indomitable tradesman
Opened his cellar looted by the Neva,
Hoping to make good his loss at his neighbour's expense.
Boats were being hauled away from courtyards.

  Already Count Khvostov, beloved of heaven,

Was singing the disaster of Neva's banks
In his immortal verses.

                    But my poor, poor
Yevgeni! . . . Alas! his confused mind could not endure
The shocks he had suffered. His ears still heard
The boom of Neva and the winds. Silently
He wandered round, filled with dreadful thoughts.
Some sort of dream tormented him. A week,
A month, went by – still he did not go home.
When the time ran out, his landlord leased
His abandoned nook to a poor poet. Yevgeni
Did not come to collect his belongings. He grew
A stranger to the world. All day he wandered
On foot, and slept at night on the embankment;
He fed on scraps handed to him through windows.
Tattered and mouldy grew his shabby clothes.
Children threw stones at him. Often the whips
Of coachmen lashed him, for he could not find his way;
It seemed he noticed nothing, deafened by
An inner turmoil. And so he dragged out his life,
Neither beast nor man, neither this nor that,
Not of the living world nor of the dead . . .

   Once he was sleeping on the Neva banks.
The days of summer were declining towards autumn.
A sickly wind was breathing. The sullen wave
Splashed against the embankment, reproachfully
Grumbling and beating against the smooth steps,
Like a petitioner at the door of judges
Who keep turning him away. The poor wretch woke.
It was dark: rain dripped, the wind howled gloomily;
A distant watchman traded cries with it.
Yevgeni started up; recalled his nightmare;

Hastily he set off wandering, until
He suddenly stopped – and slowly began to cast
His eyes around, with wild fear on his face.
He found himself at the foot of the pillars of
The great house. Over the porch the lions stood
On guard, like living creatures, with their paws
Upraised; and eminently dark and high
Above the railed-in rock, with arm outstretched,
The Image, mounted on his horse of bronze.

Yevgeni shuddered. Terribly his thoughts
Grew clear in him. He recognized the place
Where the flood played, where greedy waves had pressed,
Rioting round him angrily, and the lions,
And the square, and him who motionlessly
Held aloft his bronze head in the darkness,
Him by whose fateful will the city had
Been founded on the sea . . . How terrible
He was in the surrounding murk! What thought
Was on his brow, what strength was hidden in him!
And in that steed what fire! Where do you gallop,
Proud steed, and where will you plant your hoofs?
O mighty master of fate! was it not thus,
Towering on the precipice's brink,
You reared up Russia with your iron curb?

The poor madman walked around the pedestal
Of the Image, and brought wild looks to bear
On the countenance of the lord of half the world.
His breast contracted, his brow was pressed against
The cold railings, his eyes were sealed by mist,
Flames ran through his heart, his blood boiled.
Sombrely he stood before the statue;
His teeth clenched, his hands tightened, trembling
With wrath, possessed by a dark power, he whispered:

256

'All right then, wonder-worker, just you wait!'
And suddenly set off running at breakneck speed.
It seemed to him that the face of the dead Tsar,
Momentarily flaring up with rage,
Was slowly turning . . . Across the empty square
He runs, and hears behind him – like the rumble
Of thunder – the clash and clangor of hoofs
Heavily galloping over the shaking square.
And lit by the pale moonlight, stretching out
His hand aloft, the Bronze Horseman rushes
After him on his ponderously galloping mount;
And all night long, wherever the madman ran,
The Bronze Horseman followed with a ringing clatter.

And from that time, whenever his wanderings took him
Into that square, confusion appeared on his face.
Hastily he would press his hand to his heart,
As though to ease its torment, he would doff
His tattered cap, he would not raise his troubled
Eyes, and would go on by some roundabout way.

A small island can be seen off-shore. Sometimes
A fisherman out late will moor there with
His net and cook his meagre supper. Or
Some civil servant, boating on a Sunday,
Will pay a visit to the barren island.
No grass grows, not a blade. The flood, in sport,
Had driven a ramshackle little house there.
Above the water it had taken root
Like a black bush. Last spring a wooden barge
Carried away the wreckage. By the threshold
They found my madman, and on that very spot
For the love of God they buried his cold corpse.

[1833]

NOTES

I

39 'To Olga Masson'. Olga Masson was a well-known Petersburg *cocotte*.

44 'To the Fountain of the Palace of Bakhchisarai'. Maria and Zarema are the heroines of Pushkin's narrative poem, *The Fountain of Bakhchisarai*. Zarema, a passionate Georgian, is drowned on suspicion of having killed Maria, a Polish girl who has supplanted her in the Khan's affections. The inconsolable Khan built the fountain in memory of Maria.

47 '19 October'. The *lycée* at Tsarskoye where Pushkin studied was opened on 19 October 1811. In this remarkable poem of friendship, he makes specific reference to the following schoolfellows: Korsakov, who died in Italy in 1820; the sailor Matyushkin; Pushchin, who visited Pushkin in exile at Mikhailovskoye in 1825; Gorchakov, whom he had met by chance in the same year; the poets Delvig and Kuechelbecker (Wilhelm). It was to be another two years before Pushkin was able to join the ritual celebration: with a sadly depleted company, for Pushchin and Kuechelbecker had been sent to Siberia for their part in the Decembrist uprising of December 1825.

53 'Confession'. This refers to Alexandra Osipova, the pretty stepdaughter of Pushkin's neighbour at Mikhailovskoye, Mme Osipova. This widow's houseful of charming girls provided the poet with a welcome haven.

59 'Arion'. Like the ancient poet Arion, who escaped drowning by swimming ashore on a dolphin's back, Pushkin had miraculously avoided his friends' Siberian

fate because of his absence from Petersburg, in exile, during the Decembrist uprising.

62 'Anchar'. The exotic poison-tree (or Upas-tree) of travellers' tales. The poem reflects, in miniature, the theme of 'The Bronze Horseman': the interwoven destinies of tyrant and slave.

72 'What comfort for you in my name? . . .' Karolina Sobrańska, a celebrated Polish beauty, had asked the poet to write his name in her album.

89 '. . . I have visited again . . .'. Written after a visit to Mikhailovskoye, where his old nurse had meanwhile died.

91 'Eyes open wide, the poet weaves . . .'. From Pushkin's unfinished story, *Egyptian Nights*. An Italian *improvisatore* calls on the Petersburg poet, Charsky; the latter tests his powers of improvisation with this theme: 'The poet himself should choose the subjects for his songs. The crowd has no right to direct his inspiration.' The Italian astonishes Charsky by spontaneously declaiming this poem.

92 'Exegi monumentum'. A paraphrase of Horace's 'Exegi Monumentum'. Pushkin was following the Russian precedent of Lomonosov and Derzhavin, who had also written versions of the Horace. 'Alexander's column': the monument to Alexander I in Petersburg; though the Russian allows a secondary allusion, to the Pharos of ancient Alexandria.

II

Page
114 'The Gypsies'. The exiled poet to whom the old gypsy refers is Ovid, banished by the Emperor Augustus in A.D. 8 to Tomi on the Black Sea, not far from Bessarabia, the setting of 'The Gypsies' and Pushkin's own tem-

porary exile. The gypsy's remark that the stranger in exile 'did not understand anything' is a marvellous example both of Pushkin's subtle humour and his truth to life. To the natives, the sophisticated Roman poet *would* seem to understand nothing.

Pushkin is said to have adapted Zemfira's Song (p.116) from a genuine Moldavian gypsy song. I have used an amended version of George Borrow's translation of Zemfira's Song, written and published when he was visiting Petersburg in 1835. Borrow did not meet Pushkin, but translated four of his lyrics: the first English translations of Pushkin.

'Moscal' (p.121) is a derogatory Slavic term for a Muscovite.

140 'Count Nulin'. The Count refers to various leading actors of the French theatre: François Joseph Talma (1763–1826), a brilliant tragic actor; Mamselle Mars: the stage-name of Anne Boulet (1779–1847); and Charles Potier (1775–1838). Charles Victor Prévot, Vicomte d'Arlincourt (1789–1856) was a poet, dramatist and historical novelist.

The *Moscow Telegraph* (p.141) was noted for its articles on fashion.

157 'Mozart and Salieri'. 'Was the Vatican's builder not a murderer?': 'Salieri identifies himself not with Michelangelo the painter and sculptor but with the architect of the Vatican, the supreme edifice of the Church in whose name so many crimes have been committed' (John Bayley, *Pushkin*, 1971, p.220).

161 'The Stone Guest'. Pushkin's is the only version of the legend which makes the commander Donna Anna's husband, not her father.

248 'The Bronze Horseman'. *Mars' Field* is the name of the parade grounds of Petersburg.

'The pen of Karamzin' (p.249) is an allusion to the

monumental *History of the Russian State*, by N. M. Karamzin (1765–1826). Kolomna was then an outlying suburb.

Count Khvostov (p.255): a second-rate poet, a contemporary of Pushkin.